OTHER BOOKS BY ANNABELLA MICHAELS

Souls Of Chicago Series:

Feeding the Soul, Book 1
Music of the Soul, Book 2
Protecting the Soul, Book 3
Renewing the Soul, Book 4

DEDICATION

To Jenn, who has shown me more love, compassion, encouragement and kindness than I ever could have hoped for. Your friendship means everything to me and I feel blessed every single day that we found each other in this big, crazy world. Also, thank you for understanding that there is no man like a Greene man.

PROLOGUE

Akio

I PARKED MY CAR OUTSIDE OF THE BUILDING AND LOOKED UP AT what I was sure had been a productive manufacturing warehouse in its day, but had become nothing more than an empty shell as the years moved on. It wasn't in the best part of Chicago either, which had the hairs on the back of my neck standing up. I pulled my phone from my pocket and double-checked the address that Landon had given me, just to be sure; I was definitely in the right place. Landon had mentioned that Carter and Ryan lived in one of the abandoned buildings and had fixed it up into a beautifully designed living space, but I was having trouble picturing anything beyond the broken windows and graffiti-covered walls.

I was half an hour early for my meeting, but there was no way I was going to wander around the creepy building by myself, so I stayed in my car and locked the doors. The fact that I was even there in the first place proved that there wasn't much I wouldn't do for Landon Greene. Not only was he my boss, but he was also my best friend. We'd met when I was working as a temp at the same agency as him. The two of us hit it off right away, quickly becoming friends and he'd confided in me that he was unhappy with his job as a talent scout. He'd wanted to not only discover up-and-coming musicians, he also wanted to take them under his wing and help them navigate their way through the music industry, so that they could reach their full potential.

Landon had finally made the decision to start his own agency that would allow him to do the things he wanted and when he asked me if I would be interested in joining him as his office manager, I'd jumped at the chance. It was exactly the kind of job I'd been looking for and Landon was more than generous with my starting salary and benefits package. The best part however, was that I would get to continue working with Landon; who was not only a wonderful boss, but an incredible friend.

Landon's knack for recognizing raw talent had helped build his reputation and when he took over the management of Carter's Creed, his business had skyrocketed. He quickly became one of the most sought-after music agents and had ended up having to hire more managers to help oversee the many bands that wanted to be signed on with his agency. Landon would never hand his brother's band over to another manager though, so between preparing them for their second worldwide tour and wanting to spend more time with his fiancé, Micah, he had begun handing more of the responsibility over to me to help carry the load.

Part of that responsibility included a project that was near and dear to all our hearts, Agape House. Landon's family had always been very involved with the center for LGBTQA youth and he'd gotten me involved as soon as we'd become friends. Rylie, known to the rest of the world as Rocko, was the drummer for Carter's Creed and had started volunteering there as part of his recovery program from drug and alcohol addiction. Rylie then told Lachlan, his fiancé and owner of Golden Entertainment Studios, about the center and Lachlan decided that he needed to check it out for himself.

After meeting with the center's owner, Matt, and seeing the amazing difference Agape House was making in the lives of local LGBTQA teens, Lachlan had agreed that it was a very special place indeed, but that it needed a lot of updating. Matt had explained to him that the center depended on fundraising and the kind donations of others to stay in operation and he'd admitted to Lachlan that it was often a struggle to keep their doors open from one month to the next, which unfortunately, left no funds for upkeep on the building.

Lachlan called a meeting with the band, along with several members of the Greene family and myself, to help come up with a plan to build a new facility for the center. Lachlan was going to pay for the new building, but he also wanted to set up a fund that would keep the center running for years to come without having to struggle to make ends meet. While they had enough money between all of them to fund everything themselves, they agreed that it would be better if the community were also involved in the effort, which would bring attention to the center and what it was they were doing for the youth of Chicago.

Ryan suggested that instead of building a brand-new facility, that they look into renovating one of the old warehouses near where he and Carter lived. He pointed out that space to build was limited in the thriving city. By using one of the old warehouses they would be able to expand the center and therefore help more kids in need. Everyone agreed with Ryan's suggestion and then they began discussing fundraising ideas that would get the community involved.

It was also brought up that with the band preparing for another tour, the time that they could personally devote to the project would be limited. Kathy and Rick Greene had volunteered to head up the fundraising end of things, but they would need someone to oversee the building renovation, including meeting with contractors, electricians, and inspectors.

Landon turned in my direction and said that he didn't know

anyone with better organizational skills than me, which made me preen until I realized what he was suggesting. I told him that I had far too much work to do at the office and that I wouldn't know where to start with a project of that magnitude, but he promised to hire extra help in the office so that I could focus solely on the renovation.

Caleb added that they'd really like the person overseeing the project to be someone who was already involved with the center and cared about what happened to it, like he knew I would. I could feel my resolve crumbling and then Landon pulled out the big guns. As my best friend, he knew that flattery was my kryptonite so he reminded me of what an important role I'd played in organizing the band's first worldwide tour and that if I could handle that, then overseeing the Agape House project would be a piece of cake. Then he'd winked at me, making me glare at him in return. He knew he was going to get his way and I did too. Not only because of the flattery, but because I had a soft spot for the kids at the center.

Which was how I had ended up sitting in front of a building that looked like it could be on the set of *The Walking Dead* and wondering if I should have brought one of Micah's security guys along with me for protection from whatever might be lurking in the shadows. Landon had set up meetings with three different contractors and wanted me to decide which one would be best for the job. He hadn't told me much about any of them because he said he wanted me to make my decision based off my own impression.

A knock on the glass beside me made me scream and I clutched at my chest, attempting to keep my heart from jumping out. I turned and glared out the window, wanting to know who was responsible for trying to send me to an early grave when I was met with the most amazing pair of sea-green eyes I'd ever seen in my life. I was mesmerized by them for a few seconds, until I realized that they were also accompanied by a laughing mouth. It didn't matter that the mouth had a full bottom lip or that the teeth were perfectly straight and it didn't matter that the skin around it was perfectly golden. I saw red.

Who did the guy think he was, sneaking up on me in that kind of a neighborhood and scaring the bejeezus out of me, only to turn around and laugh about it? I should've stayed in my car because I had no idea who he was or what he might do to me, but I was too pissed off to think logically. I narrowed my eyes, hit the unlock button, and swung my door open, making him jump back or risk getting hit.

"What the hell? I don't know what you're doing in this area, but you have no business sneaking up on people and scaring them half to death," I screeched, poking my finger into his chest. I admired the fact that his t-shirt stretched nicely over his broad chest and the hardness of his pectorals under my finger tip, but that was only because I was very good at multi-tasking. His eyes widened in surprise and he held his hands up in surrender.

"I'm sorry, I didn't mean to scare you. I thought you saw me pull up beside you. I'm here for our meeting," he explained.

His words broke through my anger and it was then that I noticed the bright red Ford F-250 truck pulled up alongside my car just as he'd said. I'd been so lost in my thoughts that I hadn't even seen him. I could feel my face heating up with embarrassment when I realized that I had just yelled at the man who could possibly end up being our new contractor. Please don't let me have screwed this project up already.

"No, I'm the one who should apologize, I should have been paying better attention and then I wouldn't have been so surprised. Let's start over, shall we?" I pasted my most winning smile on my face and offered him my hand to shake. "I'm Akio Forrest."

Luckily, he didn't seem too upset because he smiled at me and slid his hand against mine. A tremor went through my hand and travelled up my arm when our skin made contact and I glanced up at his eyes, startled. He looked shocked and I wondered if he'd felt it too.

"It's nice to meet you, Akio. I'm Morgan Greene."

"Greene?" I asked curiously.

His face lit up with a smile. "Yeah, Landon's my cousin." He chuckled when he saw the surprise on my face and his cheeks dipped into a perfect set of dimples. I swallowed hard. The man was absolutely stunning. Morgan's eyes roamed over my face, settling on my lips and I felt my skin heat under his gaze. It was then that I realized I was still shaking his hand. I pulled away and cleared my throat.

"Are you ready to go inside?" I turned and walked towards the building without waiting for his response. I needed a few moments to gather myself. I'd never had that kind of reaction to another person and I wasn't sure what to make of it. I grabbed the keys out of my pocket and unlocked the heavy metal door. It made a loud screeching sound as I slowly pulled it open, wary of anything that might be living in there. Lachlan had done a walkthrough of the building before deciding to purchase it, but it was my first time there.

My eyes swept over the interior which had been stripped bare. Glass crunched under my shoes as I walked deeper into the old warehouse. Morgan let out a low whistle behind me and the sound echoed through the cavernous space. I turned to look at him, expecting him to be disgusted by what he saw, but instead he wore a look of wonder and excitement on his face. I studied him as he spun around in a slow circle, his head tilted up to take in the high ceilings and the full wall of windows.

"This is perfect," he said quietly and I looked around again, wondering what he saw in the rubble that I couldn't. He turned and headed farther into the building. I shrugged my shoulders and followed along, not really wanting to get left behind in the creepy building.

"Landon didn't tell me I was going to be meeting his cousin," I said as he pulled a tape measure from his belt loop and began measuring the windows. He kept his focus on his work as he answered.

"I probably shouldn't have said anything about it until after we discussed business, but you looked so scared out there, I just wanted to put your mind at ease. I don't want anyone claiming that your decision to hire me was biased. I'm sure that's why Landon didn't mention it."

I felt myself bristling and I narrowed my eyes at him. "You seem awfully sure that I'm going to hire you, but I'll have you know that I have several contractors to meet with and each of them are highly qualified. My decision will be made once I've met with everyone and heard what their ideas are for the center."

Morgan's tape measure snapped back into place as he turned to look at me, one brow arched. "That's exactly what you should do, but you'll still end up hiring me," he said smugly.

"And what makes you so sure?" I crossed my arms over my chest and popped a hip out. My friends told me that I had the best resting bitch face around and the moment seemed to call for it so I pulled out all the stops, but my breath caught in my throat as he moved closer. He stopped right in front of me and I was suddenly very aware of the difference between his 6' 2" frame and my own smaller 5' 7".

"I may not be the cheapest, but I promise you that I am the best man for the job." My tongue darted out to wet my lips and his eyes caught the movement. Morgan's voice was low when he spoke again. "No matter what the job is, I won't stop until everyone is completely satisfied." I felt my face heat as I caught the double meaning behind his words. His eyes raised to meet mine and he winked before turning around and continuing his work. I stood there for another moment, trying to calm my racing heart.

I followed him around for another hour as he jotted down measurements, tapped the walls and did a number of other things that I couldn't begin to understand the reasoning behind. Finally, he turned to me.

"Okay, that should about do it. I'll have plans drawn up and get back to you with my bid within the next couple of days."

"Sounds good," I told him as we walked outside. "As I said, I've got other contractors to meet with and once I have a chance to look over all the bids, I'll be in touch." I locked the door and then turned to shake his hand which was warm and just rough enough to send a tingle down my spine. It was the hand of someone who worked hard for a living and I respected that.

"It was very nice to meet you, Akio," he said and I shivered when he squeezed my hand gently. We held on just a little longer than necessary and I felt the loss when he pulled away.

"Nice to meet you too." My eyes roamed over his face for just a few seconds and then I walked to my car and climbed in. My heart was thumping wildly in my chest as I started the engine.

Morgan Greene was sexy, flirtatious and very cocky when it came to his skills as a contractor. It would be interesting to see what he came up with for the center and whether he could back up his words because regardless of the strange way my body responded to his, my only objective was building the best possible place for those kids. To do that, I would choose whoever was best for the job.

I glanced in the rearview mirror as I drove away and my eyes widened when I saw him standing beside his truck, watching me. That was the strangest encounter I'd ever experienced and I was happy to get away from him so I could figure out what in the hell had just happened. All I knew for sure was that things had just gotten very interesting.

CHAPTER
One

Akio

"SO, I'VE PUT TOGETHER THE DESIGN IDEAS FROM ALL TEN contractors, along with their bids on the project. I had the company lawyer remove the names from the papers so we wouldn't be accused of any preferential treatment from the candidates not chosen." I walked around the large conference room table, handing out the packets that I had put together for each member of the committee to review.

"That was a very smart idea," Lachlan said when I handed him a set of papers. I appreciated his praise more than he realized. I was still a little nervous about presenting my thoughts in front of this particular group of people. Not that they weren't perfectly nice and I'd gotten to know them all well enough to consider them friends, but it was a bit intimidating to be standing in front of world famous musicians, a music mogul and an ex-Navy SEAL just to name a few and know that they wanted to hear my opinion on a subject.

The only sound in the room were papers rustling as I gave them time to look over the plans in front of them. After a few minutes, I spoke. "As you can see, there were a wide variety of ideas for how to use the space as well as a broad range in prices. My recommendation would be to go with candidate number eight. Their bid rang in a little higher than most of the others, but the design ideas seem to fit most closely with what we're wanting for Agape House. They maximized the use of space so that nothing was wasted, which would allow us to serve the most kids possible. If we incorporate that design, we're looking at quadrupling the number of LGBTQA teens we'll be able to help."

"I like the layout of the kitchen area," Caleb said.

"I agree and with this design, depending on what materials are used, I think we could easily make it feel more like a home than a cafeteria," his husband, Giovanni, added. Caleb was an internationally trained chef and together they owned Romero's, one of Chicago's most popular Italian restaurants. Having their stamp of approval, particularly on the kitchen design, was huge. We continued around the table, providing each person with a chance to give their opinion and with only a few minor adjustments we were all in agreement.

"Okay then, it looks like all that's left is to show the design to Matt and if he approves, then we're ready to move forward with the project," Landon's father, Rick Greene, said. Matt was the owner of Agape House and was unfortunately unable to attend the meeting because he was short staffed that day at the center.

"I'll run them over to him as soon as we're done," I offered. "Once I have Matt's approval, I'll call the contractor and let them know they've got the job."

"So, who is our new contractor?" Carter asked.

I opened the manila envelope that contained the names of each candidate and pulled them out. My heart thudded in my chest as I read over the name of contractor number eight. I guess he hadn't been lying about being the best man for the job.

"Morgan Greene of Greene Construction," I read aloud. My answer was met with many smiles and cheers from the man's family members and I pasted a smile on my face to hide my panic. How in the hell was I supposed to get through the next several months working closely with Morgan, when I had barely gotten through our short meeting without getting completely flustered?

I busied myself with cleaning up the table as everyone began filing out of the room until eventually there was only Landon and myself left. Between his work preparing for the new world tour and me running off to meet with the contractors, it was the first time we'd been alone all week.

"How are things going with the tour plans, is everything lining up for you?" I asked.

"Going pretty well, but I miss working with you on that type of thing. Don't get me wrong, the rest of the team is great and they've been very helpful. They're just not you, you know?" I smiled at him because I did know.

From the very first day we worked together, it was obvious that Landon and I shared the same work ethic and attention to detail. As we got to know each other better and our friendship grew, we eventually got to the point where we didn't even need to say a word for the other to know what we were thinking. Micah often joked that he thought we shared a brain, but the truth was we just knew each other so well that we could anticipate what the other was going to say. Landon said it reminded him of his brother's twintuition sometimes.

As an only child, it made me happy to be able to share that close of a bond with someone else. I had lots of friends that I liked hanging out with, but Landon was different; he was like a brother to me.

"I miss it too. It feels strange to be working on separate projects," I admitted.

Other than the time that Landon left to go on tour with Carter's

Creed, we'd worked together nearly every day. I tried not to think of that time though because it was too difficult to remember that I'd almost lost him to a deranged woman who had kidnapped him and held him at gunpoint. Thankfully, Micah saved Landon and killed the woman, but not before she was able to shoot Landon in the chest, causing him to fall from a train trestle into the icy cold water below.

Landon had been left fighting for his life in the hospital. I'd wanted to be with him as he went through surgery, but I knew that he had a large family that would be by his side and the best way I could help would be to stay and take care of the company that he'd worked so hard to build. Landon told me later that I'd made the right decision, and that knowing that his agency was in good hands had allowed him to focus on his recovery without worry.

"You did a fantastic job meeting with the contractors and choosing the one that would work best for the project," Landon said, pulling me from my thoughts. "I knew you'd be perfect to head this thing up."

"Thanks, Landon. It really means a lot that you have so much confidence in me," I told him sincerely.

"Of course, I do. You're the most capable person I've ever worked with and you have great people skills which will come in very handy when dealing with all of the builders and inspectors that go along with a project this size," he replied.

"Ugh! Don't remind me." Landon chuckled as I rolled my eyes. The thought of all the red tape I'd have to get through could become overwhelming if I let it, but I'd decided to take it one day at a time. Besides, if the contractor did his job right, then it would cut down on any potential issues with the building and zoning inspectors.

"Just leave your sass at home and you should be fine," Landon teased.

I gave him a look of mock indignation. "Me, sassy? You must be mistaken. I am perfectly lovely to be around all of the time." Landon laughed loudly at that and I set the papers down on the table and glared at him, folding my arms in front of me. "When have I ever been less than pleasant? I dare you to name one time," I demanded.

"Oh, I don't know. How about the time you told that taxi driver that you would be happy to recommend a store where he could buy some deodorizer for his cab?" Landon raised an eyebrow as he waited for my response.

I wrinkled my nose at the memory. "It smelled like a musty gym bag. I was merely trying to save the good people of Chicago from enduring the olfactory horror that I had been subjected to."

"Okay, what about the time you told the couple sitting next to us at that restaurant that you had some great porn videos you could loan them if they were that interested in your sex life?" Landon challenged. I had to fight a laugh as I remembered the look on their faces.

"You know as well as I do that they were listening to our conversation. They kept glaring at us and the woman began choking when I mentioned my prostate. They should thank me for making such a generous offer, some of those videos are irreplaceable," I stated haughtily.

"Fine, what about the time…"

"I said to name one," I cut him off before he could finish his sentence and we both started laughing.

"I think I made my point. It's a good thing Morgan is an easy-going kind of guy; it'll make everything run much smoother." Landon chuckled. My laughter died out at the mention of his cousin.

"Why didn't you ever mention Morgan before?" I asked.

Landon shrugged his shoulders. "I probably have and you just don't remember. I've got twenty-two cousins. I have trouble keeping track of all of them, so I'm not surprised if you couldn't." I nodded my head and turned my attention back to my work.

"Are you two close?" I asked, trying to sound casual. I tapped the stack of papers on the table in front of me to straighten them and then slid them back into the large envelope.

"Morgan and I were very close growing up. In fact, he was the closest to me out of all my cousins. He grew up in Tennessee so I didn't get to see him as much as I would've liked, but my family owns a cabin there and every summer Mom would load us up in the car and we'd spend a few weeks there with Morgan and his mom. Our mothers may have become family through their husbands, but the two of them are thick as thieves." Landon laughed at some memory and I felt myself smiling. I loved seeing him so relaxed and happy; much different than the man he was before Micah came along.

"Anyway, my sisters were always off doing their thing and of course Caleb and Carter are two peas in a pod so that left me and Morgan to find something to entertain ourselves with. We never had a problem with that," Landon chuckled.

"We'd spend hours swimming in the creek that ran behind the cabin. This one time, Morgan got the bright idea to hang a tire swing from a nearby tree. We had a blast swinging out and then jumping down into the water, until the rope broke and Morgan fell hard. He ended up breaking his arm and had to spend the rest of the trip in a cast, so we couldn't swim anymore—not that our moms would've let us anyway. They were pretty mad about the whole thing," Landon said with a laugh. I could hear the affection he had for his cousin in his voice.

"Why did he bid on a job in Chicago if he lives in Tennessee?" I asked.

"He doesn't live there anymore, he moved to a place right outside of Chicago about a month ago. Mom said it was because he wanted to grow his business and there just wasn't enough work in the small town he grew up in, but I don't know…" His voice trailed off and I leaned forward, wishing he'd finish his thought, but then he shook his head as if to clear it and smiled at me. "Whatever the reason, I'm glad he's here and that he got the job. He's an amazing guy."

"Yeah, he's definitely something," I murmured as I began pushing the chairs in around the table. When I was finished, I looked up and found Landon studying me with his head tilted to the side.

"Why are you so interested in Morgan?" he asked.

"No reason. I just thought it would be a good idea to get to know the man I'll be working with on the project." It was an honest enough statement, but it wasn't the only reason I wanted to know more about Morgan Greene. However, there was no way I was going to admit to Landon that I hadn't been able to stop thinking about his cousin since our first meeting or wondering about the strange chemistry between us. I knew that Landon wouldn't have a problem with the fact that I found Morgan attractive, there just wasn't anything to tell. For all I knew, there may be no spark at all the second time around, but I was anxious to see him and find out.

The look Landon gave me told me that he knew there was more to it than that, but I held the envelope up in the air and gave him a broad smile. "I better get over to Agape House right away so Matt can approve the plans and we can move forward with the project."

"Okay, sounds good. Let me know if there's anything you need from me along the way. I've been busy getting everything lined up for the tour, but I don't want you to feel like you've taken the whole project on by yourself. Agape House means the world to all of us and we want to help out as much as possible."

"I know and I appreciate that. I'll keep in touch," I promised. I gave him a quick hug and then went to my desk to grab my car keys before heading out the door. I'd let Matt look over everything, but I couldn't imagine him not liking Morgan's ideas for the center.

Matt was in a meeting when I arrived at Agape House so I left the papers with Isaac, the front desk manager, who promised to give them to Matt and have him call me as soon as he got the chance. I spent about an hour visiting with the kids and helping them with their homework, before leaving for the day.

My stomach was growling as I climbed in my car and I remembered that I hadn't eaten anything since breakfast. I'd been too nervous about giving my presentation to the rest of the group to even consider eating lunch and my stomach was making its displeasure clear. My phone rang as I was contemplating whether I felt like stopping at the store to get something to make for dinner or if I would rather just pick something up from a restaurant. I smiled when I saw who it was and I pressed the button on my steering wheel to accept the call as I pulled away from the curb.

"Hey, Mama!"

"Musuko!" she answered. Warmth spread through me at the sound of my mother's gentle voice. Rena Kimura had been born and raised in Japan by very traditional parents. When she was eighteen years old, she met my father, Henry, who was there on business with the marketing company that he was interning for. According to them, it was love at first sight and despite the objections from her parents that she was being too hasty, she left with Henry when he returned to the States. They were married after only knowing each other for two months, but as they told me many times over the years, "When you meet the person that is the other half to your whole, there's no sense in wasting time."

My mother had adopted many American traditions throughout the years, but she'd also felt it was important to teach me how to speak Japanese so that I would be able to stay in touch with that part of my heritage. It never failed to make me feel special whenever she called me musuko, the Japanese term for son.

"Your father is getting ready to put some steaks on the grill and we were hoping you might stop by and have dinner with us," she offered.

"That sounds perfect, actually. I was just trying to figure out what to do for dinner," I told her.

"Great! We'll see you soon then. Be safe driving, Musuko."

"I will, Mama. Tell dad not to burn the steaks this time," I joked.

"I could try, but it wouldn't work," she said in a whisper, making me laugh. It was a long-standing joke between my mother and me. My dad loved to cook and he was actually quite good at it as long as he stayed in the kitchen, but put the man in front of an open flame and whatever he was cooking came out looking like charcoal briquettes and tasting even worse. He was always so happy doing it though that neither one of us had the heart to tell him, so we smiled and choked down the brittle substance year after year.

My parents lived just outside the city limits so it didn't take me long to arrive and I chuckled when I smelled something burning as I walked towards the house. I was very close to my parents and it was rare for me to go more than a day or two without at least talking to one of them on the phone, but I'd been swamped with work and so I hadn't spoken to them in over a week.

We enjoyed a wonderful meal, despite the charred meat, and we caught up with everything that had been going on with each other. Mom worked as a preschool teacher, not because she needed the money, but because she enjoyed being around young children. She once told me that if we wanted to make the world more loving and accepting of others, then we needed to start with our young. Dad had continued working at the same marketing company for several years until he decided to start one of his own, a choice that had turned out to be very profitable. They had each taught me the value of hard work.

After dinner, we worked together to clean up the dishes. We were laughing at a story my dad was telling about a guy that worked for him when my phone chimed, letting me know I had a text. Pulling it out of my pocket, I saw that it was from Matt. Swiping the screen with my thumb, I scanned his message.

"What has you smiling so much, Akio?" I glanced up at my dad and shrugged, shoving my phone back into my pocket.

"Nothing really, just got the go-ahead from the center's owner, saying that he approved of the plans. I better get going, I need to call the contractor and let him know that his bid has been accepted." I kissed both of them and then practically ran to my car. I was excited to be moving forward on the project, but the rapid thumping in my chest and the slight shaking of my hands had more to do with the call I was about to make than the text I had just received.

CHAPTER
Two

Morgan

I LET MY FINGERS GRAZE THE HARD SURFACE, CHECKING FOR ANY roughness as I bent down and pursed my lips, blowing gently along the length of the wood. I watched as the sawdust lifted and swirled in the sunlight streaming through the windows, the fragrant scent of oak permeating the air. I'd worked tirelessly over the last month, setting up my new place and making it into my own, but inside my workshop, surrounded by my tools and new and old pieces of wood with endless possibilities, was where I felt most at home.

I knew with my very first job, working as an intern at my dad's law firm, that I wasn't cut out for a career that would force me to sit behind a desk for eight hours a day. I'd always been the type who needed to be moving and doing things. I loved working with my hands, building things from scratch or taking old things and making them into something new and beautiful again. It wasn't until a friend of mine talked me into working with him on a construction site one summer that I found my true calling. I worked my ass off and learned as much as I could until I was finally able to start my own company.

What started out as me and a couple of buddies, soon turned into a thirty-person operation. I was proud of the work I'd done and I was happy with the level of success I'd achieved. It hadn't been an easy decision to leave Tennessee, but I was excited about living closer to my cousins and I was fairly confident that moving my business to a large city such as Chicago would prove to be fortuitous.

My friend John, who was an engineer in Chicago, had been invaluable in helping me find new crew members and he said that he knew plenty of skilled people that would be eager to work for me as soon as I needed them. All I needed was the green light on the Agape House project and I'd be ready to move forward. I had confidence in my ability to do the best job, but you never knew how those things would go. I'd been on pins and needles for the last week and it was making me crazy, but there was nothing I could do but wait.

I finished sanding down the table I was building and satisfied that it no longer had any rough edges, I began cleaning up the mess I'd made. I smiled as I moved around, sweeping the floors and putting things back where they belonged. The barn which had been used by the previous owner to store his antique cars was perfect for a woodworking shop. Wooden cabinets lined an entire wall and offered plenty of storage for all my odds and ends and I'd hung pegboard for my tools to hang from.

There was also an old workbench that had been the man's grandfather's, but had no place in the Florida condo he was moving to so he'd sold it with the house. I liked to run my hands over it, feeling the smoothness that could only come from years of use and imagined his grandfather as a craftsman, much like my own grandfather had been. Some of my fondest memories were of spending time with my grandpa in his shop, watching him as he worked. Every night he would sit out on his front porch and whittle. He said it relaxed his mind after a busy day and he'd bought me my own knife on my tenth birthday so that I could whittle with him. I was never as good at it as he was, but it was because of my grandpa that I had developed my love of crafting things out of wood.

I may have been moving my business to the city, but I was a country boy through and through. I knew that I wouldn't enjoy living in a busy city so I'd asked the realtor to look for something on the outskirts of Chicago. My list of demands was fairly straight forward; I needed a place that I could use as a workshop and enough land that I wouldn't feel like my neighbors were right on top of me. What she found was even better than I'd hoped for. A newly built log cabin, sitting on twelve acres, complete with woods, a pond, and, of course, the barn. It was my own little piece of paradise and I loved every square inch of it.

When I'd finished cleaning up, I headed to the house to take a shower. I'd been so busy getting everything set up at my new place that I hadn't had time to see my family, so when Landon had called that morning and asked if I could meet him for dinner, I'd jumped at the chance. I was disappointed that Micah wouldn't be there because I was eager to get to know the man that had captured my cousin's heart, but Landon had explained that Micah was working a case so he wouldn't be there. I was looking forward to catching up with Landon though. We had always been very close and talked at least once or twice each week on the phone, but it wasn't the same as actually being in the same room as each other, which was a big reason why I had decided to move there in the first place.

I came from a huge family with loads of cousins, but somehow my parents had only ended up with me. I knew they'd tried to have more kids, but it just wasn't possible. Mom always told me that I was her miracle baby and more than she could've ever wished for. I knew I was lucky to have the parents I had, but a part of me had always wished for a sister or brother that I could grow up with. Landon had filled that role for me, even though we didn't live together. I couldn't imagine any two brothers being closer than he and I were which was why it had been so scary when I thought I was going to lose him.

I already knew that I had to get out of the town I grew up in, I just wasn't sure where I was going to go. Hearing that Landon had come so close to death at the hands of a psychotic woman had been the deciding factor and I'd quickly called my realtor and set things in motion. I looked up at my new house as I climbed the steps and smiled; moving to Illinois had been the right choice. Being in a new place, surrounded by my crazy, loving family was just what I needed.

My phone rang as I was washing my hands so I quickly dried them off and pulled my phone from my pocket. My heart thudded in my chest when I saw the name displayed on the screen. *Akio Forrest.*

"Hello?" I said. I hoped my voice didn't sound as nervous as I felt. Despite my cocky attitude when I'd met Akio, I was very anxious to hear what he had to say. I had no doubts that I could get plenty of other jobs in the city if that one didn't pan out, but none of them would be as worthwhile as the Agape House project nor would they get my business name out there as quickly as that would.

"Hi! Is this Morgan Greene?" Akio asked and just like that my stomach flipped for a completely different reason. An image of the man came to mind and I recalled how he'd stunned me the first time I'd laid eyes on him.

I'd climbed out of my truck and approached the man sitting in the little blue Toyota Prius. I'd assumed, since he was the only one around, that he was the person I was there to meet. He didn't move as I neared so I tapped on his window to get his attention. I couldn't help but laugh at the startled expression on his face as he turned towards me and grabbed his chest. He'd obviously been so lost in his thoughts that he hadn't heard me arrive.

Before I knew what was happening, he swung the door open, climbed out of his car, and began yelling at me. I barely heard his words though or felt his finger poking into my chest as I stared down at the most breathtaking man I'd ever seen. He had black hair that even styled, still flopped down slightly over his forehead and the most adorable freckles that dotted his upturned nose. His brown eyes, which narrowed slightly at the corners, were framed by thick lashes. His bottom lip was fuller than the top, making it look like he was wearing a constant pout and I had the sudden urge to reach out and run my finger over his cheek to see if his skin was as smooth and silky as it appeared.

"Hello? Are you still there?" I heard Akio say and I realized that I'd never answered his question.

"Yes, I'm here. This is Morgan," I said in a rush.

"Oh, good. This is Akio Forrest. I'm the one that met with you about the Agape House project," he supplied.

"I remember who you are," I answered, as if I could ever forget. There was a slight pause on his end and then I heard him clear his throat.

"So, I met with the rest of the group today to go over the bids from each of the candidates for the job and then I showed the ideas to Matt, the owner of Agape House, to get his final approval and we've come to a unanimous decision. We were very impressed with your design ideas as well as the timeframe you set up in order to complete the project and we would like to offer you the job, if you are still interested."

"That's terrific, thank you very much." I let out the breath I'd been holding and answered as calmly as possible while pumping my fist in the air. Akio chuckled and I wondered if I hadn't sounded as calm as I'd intended.

"Good. How much time will you need to get everything set up? We'd like to get moving on this as soon as possible," he explained.

"I understand," I said, nodding my head as if he could see the movement through the phone. "I already have several crew members on standby, I just need to make a few phone calls and I should be good to go."

"Perfect. Are you available on Monday? I'd like to do a walk through with Matt there so we can make sure that everyone's on the same page before we begin," he suggested.

"That's a good idea. I'm available all day," I told him.

"In that case, maybe we could go afterwards to get you set up at the local builder's supply warehouse. Lachlan set up a line of credit so you'll be able to order new supplies whenever you need without having to wait on him. I'll need to go with you to add you to the approved list of people allowed to use the line of credit," Akio explained. "If there's anything else you need from me, don't hesitate to ask. This is the best number to reach me because I almost always have my phone on me."

"Sounds good. Thank you, Akio. I'm looking forward to working with you," I said.

"I'm looking forward to it too," he answered.

It wasn't until we'd hung up that I realized how late it had gotten. I was going to have to hurry if I didn't want to be late meeting Landon. I smiled as I started the water for my shower. Everything in my life seemed to be falling into place: a beautiful home, new job, and a sexy man that I was going to get to work with. It seemed like we would have a lot to celebrate that night.

The parking lot was full outside of the sports bar and grill that Landon had chosen to meet at and I wondered if there was a big game going on or if the place always drew such a big crowd. I waited patiently as the driver of an SUV vacated his spot before I pulled in and parked my truck. I locked up and made my way to the front door, smiling when I saw Landon waiting outside. He was looking down at his phone and wearing a goofy grin on his face and I would've bet money that he was texting Micah. I cleared my throat as I got nearer and his head jerked up in surprise, his smile spreading when he realized it was me.

"Morgan!" he exclaimed, throwing his arms around me and engulfing me in a warm hug. I hugged him back, not caring who might be watching. That was one thing all of us Greenes had in common; we were very affectionate people and we had no problem showing it.

"It's good to see you," I said as we took a step back so we could look each other over. He looked better than I'd seen him in a long time. The tense set of his jaw was gone, replaced by a relaxed smile. Landon was obviously very happy and I was thrilled for him. My cousins were all amazing people and I was so happy that they'd each found their soulmates.

"It's good to see you too. I was beginning to wonder if it was ever going to happen though," he teased.

"I'm sorry. I've been trying to get everything set up with my new house before I started working again, but I promise, I'm going to have all of you out soon to see the place."

"I understand, we've all been busy too getting everything ready for the new tour. I just like to give you a hard time," Landon said with a cheeky grin. I gave him a playful punch to the arm and we laughed as I followed him inside.

It was loud inside as fans drank their beers and cheered on their favorite teams. There were large screen TVs mounted all around the place, allowing every person to partake in whichever sport they chose to watch. Nearly every table was taken, but we were able to find a spot near the back of the restaurant which was fine with me because it got us away from some of the noise so we'd be able to talk.

"Sorry, I didn't realize when I chose this place that the Bulls were playing tonight," Landon said as he slid into the booth and glanced around. "Or that there was a huge pay-per-view fight going on apparently," he continued with a laugh. "Would you rather go somewhere else?" he offered.

"Do they have good food here?" I asked. Landon answered with a nod. "Beer?" He nodded again with a smirk. "Then this is perfect," I stated. We placed an order of wings and beer with the waitress and then smiled at each other.

"You look happier than I've seen in a long time. I take it being engaged agrees with you?" I said with a smirk.

A wide grin split his face as he answered. "Being engaged to *Micah* agrees with me," he corrected then shook his head. "I never thought I'd meet someone who was so perfect for me, but Micah is everything I've ever wanted. He knows what I need before I do sometimes and there's nothing I can't say to him. He really is my best friend and I can't wait to marry him." My smile grew as he continued telling me about his fiancé.

"I'm so happy for you, Landon. Micah sounds like an incredible person and I can't wait to get to know him," I said sincerely.

"I want that too. Although, I'm sure Micah feels like he already knows you with as much as I talk about you."

"I hope you've only told him the good parts," I joked and Landon laughed.

"Don't worry, good things are all I can remember with you." Warmth filled my chest when he said that. My favorite childhood memories were of my times spent with my cousins and I was so glad that I had made the move to be closer to them, giving us an opportunity to get to know each other better as adults. The waitress brought our food then and we were quiet as we both dug in.

"So, tell me about you. How are you doing and what made you finally decide to move to Chicago? Mom told me it was because there wasn't enough work for you back there, but I know better. It seemed like every time we talked on the phone, you were just getting home from work," Landon said after a few moments.

"It was just time for a change and I wanted to be closer to you guys, you know that," I responded casually. Landon tilted his head and studied me without saying anything. I took a long pull from my beer and then set it back down with a sigh. "What do you want to know?" I knew my cousin well enough to know that he wasn't going to give up until he got to the truth.

Landon folded his arms and placed them on the table as he leaned towards me. "None of it makes sense. Why would you leave a lucrative business behind just to try and start it up somewhere else and why did you come alone? Where's David?" I waited for the pain to come at the sound of his name, but as usual there was nothing but regret and a hint of anger, both at David and myself. I pushed my basket of food away, no longer hungry.

"David and I aren't together anymore. I found out he'd been cheating on me," I told him.

"What the hell? That motherfucker!" Landon said, sitting up straight in his seat.

"It wasn't all his fault." Landon gave me an incredulous look and opened his mouth, but I held my hand up to stop him. "Trust me, I was plenty pissed when I found out about his affair and I still think it was a shitty thing to do, but once I got over the initial shock, I started to really think about it and I realized some things about our relationship and about myself."

"Like what?" Landon asked gently.

"Like the fact that we should've never tried to turn our friendship into something more. We'd known each other since high school and we got along great. We liked the same movies and we laughed at the same jokes. We both liked being outdoors and doing things like exploring caves and bungee jumping, but there was nothing else there, no spark, no connection. We were just friends with mutual interests." I stared down at the bottle I held between my hands and traced the moisture running down the side with my thumb.

"David knew something was missing and he tried to tell me. I didn't realize it at the time, I thought he was just nagging me, but after I found out about him and that guy, I realized he'd been trying to tell me for a long time in his own way." I looked up at Landon, catching his sympathetic gaze.

"I hear the way you talk about Micah and the way your face lights up at just the mention of his name and I realized that I never felt any of that with David. Hell, I've never felt that with any of the guys I've been with. Maybe I just don't feel things the same way other people do. I mean, I walked in and found David with another man in our shower and all I felt was anger that he would go behind my back like that. I waited to be hit with a crippling pain that should come with something like that, but it never did and it scared the shit out of me." I shook my head, frustrated with myself.

"We ended things that day and David ended up moving in with the guy. I heard through the small-town grapevine that they were planning on getting married. That was when I decided it was time for a change. I just couldn't stay there and be reminded of my failures."

"You didn't fail. It's never wrong to give love a chance," Landon said. "And there's nothing wrong with you," he stated, holding my gaze intently. "I know you, Morgan, I've known you my whole life and I know what a loving and wonderful man you are. The fact that you weren't devastated by what David did doesn't mean that there's something wrong with you, it just means that David wasn't *the one*. If he had been, you'd have felt like your heart had been put through a shredder when you found out he'd been cheating. You have so much love to give and when you find that special person, your soulmate, then you'll be flooded with feelings for them. You'll see."

"I don't think I have a soulmate out there, but either way, I think I'm happy just having fun for now," I told him, picking up my beer and taking a drink.

"Fair enough. You have your fun, but when you meet the man who grabs your heart and won't let go, I'm going to be there to say I told you so," Landon said with a smug grin.

"Whatever," I laughed. "Enough with the heavy shit, I have good news I wanted to share with you."

"What could it possibly be?" Landon's smug grin grew wider.

"You already know, don't you?" I rolled my eyes, making Landon laugh.

"I was there when the group chose your bid. All we were waiting on was Matt's approval and I knew there was no way he wouldn't love the plans you came up with. Congratulations, you're the perfect man for the job."

"Thanks, Landon. I'm really excited to get started."

"Your designs were incredible and the use of space was brilliant. I already knew how good you were at your job so I wasn't surprised when Akio recommended you. I could tell you made a huge impression on him. He couldn't stop asking questions about you." My heart thudded at Landon's words.

"Really? What all did he want to know?" The waitress brought another round of beers for each of us and I took a drink of mine, trying to appear casual. Landon didn't need to know that I thought his best friend was sexy as hell.

"He just asked if we were close and if I knew why you'd moved here. That kind of thing."

"What did you tell him?" I asked.

Landon narrowed his eyes at me. "Why are you so curious about Akio?"

I shrugged. "I just thought it would be a good idea to know more about the man I'll be working with, that's all," I replied.

"Funny, those were almost his exact same words when I asked him that question. Seems curious that you both were asking so many questions about each other. Makes me wonder what exactly happened during your first meeting," Landon said, sounding suspicious.

"Nothing happened. It was strictly business so don't go getting any ideas, okay?" I warned.

Landon laid a hand on his chest and gave me a look of pure innocence. "I'm sure I have no idea what you're talking about," he drawled and I couldn't help but laugh at his horrible impression of a Southern belle.

"Uh huh, I hear you. Why don't you quit worrying about who I'm attracted to and start telling me about your wedding plans," I said. Landon's eyes grew wide and his jaw dropped. It took me a few seconds to replay my last words in my head and I realized what I'd basically admitted to. My shoulders slumped as I waited for Landon to say something. What he said surprised me.

"I'm not going to give you a hard time about this. Just know that if something were to happen between the two of you, I'd be perfectly fine with it, okay? You both are extremely important to me."

"Thanks, but really, I don't think anything's going to happen. Like I told you, I'm not looking for anything right now."

"Okay, I get it. I won't butt in, I just thought you should know that. When Micah and I were first starting out, we had to keep things quiet because he was worried about how Giovanni would feel about him hooking up with his brother-in-law. I don't want you to have the same worries if something like that would happen with you two."

"Thanks, Landon. You're a really good guy." I smiled at him. "Now, can we change the subject please?" I teased and Landon laughed.

We spent the rest of the evening talking about his wedding and catching up with each other. When I went to bed that night, I was still wearing a smile on my face. My relationship with David had only lasted a year, but it wasn't until it ended that I realized how unsettled I'd felt throughout it all. Moving to Chicago and starting over had been the right decision for me and I was looking forward to the next chapter in my life.

CHAPTER
Three

Akio

I SPENT ALL DAY SATURDAY RUNNING ERRANDS AND TAKING CARE of the things I didn't have time for during the week. I placed my clothes in the back seat of my car and then climbed in as I mentally checked off the things I'd already accomplished. I'd already been to the grocery store, the post office, had my hair cut, and picked up my dry cleaning.

Even though I'd just bought groceries, I didn't feel like cooking anything at home so I decided to run by Romero's and pick something up on my way home. I was meeting some friends of mine at our favorite club and I wanted time to shower and pick out the perfect outfit to wear. I may have just been hanging out with my friends, but that didn't mean I couldn't look good while I did it.

It didn't take me long to get to Romero's and I pulled up alongside the curb and parked. The restaurant was as busy as ever as I stepped inside, but I spotted Lauren, Giovanni's assistant manager, across the room. She was a beautiful woman and would stand out in any crowd. She glanced up as I walked in the door and waved then motioned for me to go on back before returning her attention to the customers she'd been chatting with.

I made my way through the crowded dining room towards the door that led into the kitchen. Caleb and Giovanni had both insisted that I be treated just like the rest of their family when I was there, and that meant going to the kitchen and helping myself to the food. They wouldn't let me pay for anything either, but I'd long since given up on trying to argue with either one of them.

A heavenly mixture of garlic, oregano, butter, and tomatoes had my mouth watering as I walked into the kitchen and I closed my eyes and inhaled deeply. The sound of someone laughing had my eyes popping open and I found Curtis chuckling as he stirred a big pot on the stove. Curtis had been hired by Caleb and Giovanni to help with the cooking and to allow them time away from the restaurant, something that had been needed more and more once they'd adopted their daughter, Sarah.

Curtis was a friendly guy; good looking, funny, and sweet. He was also an amazing chef, nearly as good as Caleb. I glanced over at Marco, the kitchen manager who had his back to me. I could see his shoulders shaking and knew that I had provided them both with amusement. However, I wasn't surprised because the same thing happened every time I went there. I couldn't help it; the smells were just too enticing.

"Go ahead and laugh it up, guys. I can't help it that your cooking is divine. I don't want to gain a hundred pounds though so I savor the smell instead," I said with a huff. Marco let out a loud bark of laughter, no longer trying to spare my feelings.

"You are just too much." He was grinning as he shook his head.

"You're not the first person to say that to me," I replied saucily, placing my hands on my hips and arching a brow. My statement was followed by more laughter which I soon joined. I loved going there and seeing those guys. No matter what kind of mood I was in when I arrived, I always left with a smile from bantering back and forth with the two of them.

"Are you hungry, Akio? You want me to make you a plate of your favorite?" Curtis asked. I thought about getting my usual order of fettucine Alfredo, but decided against it. I'd been blessed with a fast metabolism that allowed me to eat pretty much anything I wanted without gaining weight, a fact that my friends were all envious of, but I figured I should probably stick with something lighter that night.

"I'm starving, but I just want a salad to take home, please," I replied.

"A salad? Boy, are you feeling alright?" I laughed at the bewildered look Marco was giving me.

"I feel fine, I promise," I assured him. "I'm going out with some friends tonight. I'll be dancing and drinking and none of that goes well with a full stomach."

"Ahhh, a night out on the town, huh? Maybe you could talk Curtis into going out sometime. I keep telling him he needs to get out more, meet a guy his age that he could have fun with. He's too young to be working so hard all the time." Marco raised his voice on that last part as he stared pointedly at the younger man. I could tell by the way Curtis rolled his eyes, that it was an argument they'd had on more than one occasion.

"I go out, but I have responsibilities here too," Curtis interjected.

"G and Caleb would give you any night off you wanted so don't use that as an excuse. Besides, when's the last time you went out?" Marco challenged. I figured it would be best to keep my mouth shut so I did just that, letting my eyes dart back and forth between them as if I were watching a tennis match. Curtis mumbled something, but it was too low for me to hear.

"What was that?" Marco asked, not letting it go.

"I said three months ago, okay? Are you happy now?" Curtis exclaimed, sounding exasperated.

"Oh my God! Why?" I said before I could stop myself. I couldn't imagine going that long without going out and having a good time. Maybe Marco had a point; Curtis was much too young to be staying at home every night. Especially if he didn't have a sexy man waiting for him there.

Curtis's shoulders slumped. "I went out a few months ago and met a guy. He was funny and nice and built like a god. We had a great time, spent an amazing night together, and I thought we really connected, you know? He asked for my number the next morning and said he wanted to see me again, but he never called. I haven't really felt like going out since then."

"I'm sorry, man," Marco said sympathetically. "I never would've given you such a hard time if I'd known. I just want you to be happy."

"I know that and I appreciate it," Curtis said with a shy smile.

"I know you're working tonight, but why don't you and I go out the next time you're off," I offered. Curtis was a cool guy and I knew he'd have fun with my friends. Maybe a night of hanging out and dancing our asses off would get his mind off that guy.

"That's a great idea!" Marco exclaimed excitedly. "You two should double date. You could each pick a guy for the other one, that way there's no pressure to find a date for yourself. Great suggestion, Akio." I whipped my head in his direction, not quite sure what had just happened and found him smiling smugly. My eyes narrowed at him. The older man was shrewder than I'd realized because he'd just put me in a position that he knew I wouldn't be able to back out of. At least not without hurting Curtis's feelings and there was no way I'd do that.

"That would be awesome!" Curtis said, sounding excited. "I'm sure you'll pick someone great and with you there, it won't feel as awkward as a lot of blind dates can be." My mouth was still slack as he turned his attention back to the stove and began stirring whatever was in the pot. "I'm off on Monday. Is that enough time for you to find someone for me?" he said over his shoulder.

"Sure," I said in a daze. Marco handed me a to-go bag and I blessed him with one of my most heated glares, but he just clapped me on the shoulder and chuckled to himself.

"I'm looking forward to this, Akio. Thanks a lot for thinking of it," Curtis said as I opened the door.

"No problem," I murmured. I could still hear Marco's quiet laughter as the door swung shut. *What in the hell have I just gotten myself into?*

"Hey, Akio! Let us in," I heard Travis yell right before someone started banging loudly on my door. I raced to open it before one of my neighbors called the building manager to complain.

"You do remember that I have neighbors, right?" I said by way of greeting. I held the door open as my three friends brushed past me into my apartment.

"How could we forget? She was eyeing us through the crack in her door the whole time," Garrett responded, rolling his eyes.

"So, you just had to poke the bear and start banging on my door?" I asked. I shut the door and then followed them into the living room, watching as they made themselves at home.

Travis was blond, blue-eyed, and a notorious flirt. He had broad shoulders, sculpted arms, and a six-pack of abs that made all the boys salivate. He'd been captain of his high school baseball and basketball teams and had started out playing for the college. Travis soon discovered that he had interests beyond sports though and, against his father's wishes, had quit the team and pursued a major in physical therapy instead. Other than his career and friendship with the three of us, he didn't take anything very seriously and as far as I could remember, had never left the bar alone when we went out.

Garrett had dark brown hair that was cut shorter on the sides and longer on the top and beautiful gray eyes that shone out from behind the thick black frames he wore. He was the dreamer of our group. He majored in literature, but instead of becoming a teacher like both of his parents, he'd decided to try his hand at writing. Garrett quickly became very successful as a contemporary gay romance author and had recently published the final book in his third series.

Jasper was the quietest of the four of us. He had been an art major in college and while many of the art students dressed in an emo style, as if they were playing a part, it was clear that the way he dressed was simply an extension of his personality. Black jeans and t-shirt, black Converse shoes that he had decorated with a silver permanent marker, and leather cuffs around each wrist. He was a tiny wisp of a guy and we were all very protective of him. He'd come a long way over the years in opening up to us, but we knew that there was a lot he kept hidden. Shortly before graduation, Jasper got a job as a tattoo artist and was hoping to open his own shop one day.

The four of us had met as freshmen at the University of Chicago and became fast friends. Looking at us, it seemed unlikely that the four of us would've become friends, but somehow, we'd just clicked and there wasn't anything we wouldn't do for each other.

"Mrs. Stevenson always seems creepy the way she watches you," Travis replied, pulling me from my thoughts as he plopped down on my couch and threw his feet up on the coffee table.

"You should try being nice," I suggested, leaning down to swat his feet off the furniture.

"Why? Because that's worked so well for you?" Jasper raised a brow at me, daring me to argue, but I shrugged my shoulders instead.

He had a point really. I'd tried to get along with the older lady when I'd first moved in, bringing her mail to her when I went down to get my own and offering to pick stuff up for her from the grocery store. She'd always just stare at me though, not saying a word, and nothing I did had made her warm up to me.

Eventually I'd stopped trying, resigned to the fact that we were just not meant to get along, but I still hated it and couldn't help but wonder if maybe she wasn't just lonely. In the four years since I'd moved in, I'd never seen anyone stop by to visit her.

"Where are we headed tonight?" I asked, making my way into the kitchen and pulling a bottle of water from the fridge.

"Lush-Us!" my friends answered in unison, making me laugh. I wasn't surprised by their response. Chicago offered a great night life, but Lush-Us was by far our favorite club. The bartenders were friendly, the male dancers were sexy, and the drinks went down way too smooth. I was in the mood to dance that night so I quickly agreed.

I went to my bedroom and grabbed a jacket from my closet, pausing to check myself in the mirror one last time. I'd chosen to wear a tight pair of red jeans that I'd recently purchased because I liked the way they showed off my ass and a tight black button-up shirt with the sleeves rolled up part way. A pair of black boots completed the ensemble. My friends often teased me about what they referred to as my "runway requirements," but I didn't think I was that bad. I simply preferred to look my best no matter what the occasion. When I looked good, I felt good and on that particular night, I was feeling fabulous.

I played around with my hair for a moment, trying to get an errant strand to lie where it should, but no matter what I tried, it immediately flopped back down. I had just given up with a sigh when I noticed movement behind me in the mirror. Garrett stood in the doorway of my room, his hands shoved in his pockets as he stared at me. I turned to him with my hands on my hips.

"If you're here to give me hell about my fashion sense, you can stop right there. It takes work to look this good," I said, moving my hands down my body. I waited for Garrett's laugh, but it never came. His eyes followed the movement of my hands and he swallowed hard.

"You…you do look good, very good," he stuttered. Perhaps it

was the low lighting of my bedroom, but it looked like he was blushing and I had no idea why.

"Oh! Well, thanks," I responded lamely. "You okay, buddy? Is something wrong? Do you have writer's block again? Because I'd be willing to talk it out with you, I think I was pretty helpful last time," I said with a smirk. Garrett laughed that time and I felt my shoulders relax. I hated to see my friends upset.

"My characters are talking to me just fine, thank you, and if I remember correctly, I vetoed your suggestion that my character who was a teacher have an orgy with the male students in his class," Garrett said, shaking his head.

"I said it should be after school hours," I tossed back at him with mock indignation. I hadn't been serious about my suggestion, but I knew that talking with him about his characters would help Garrett to get ideas flowing and it worked because two weeks later he called to let me now that he'd finished his novel.

"It would have been unethical and my character was a nice guy," he explained with an exasperated shake of his head.

"It would've been fucking hot though," I said, wagging my brows at him.

"Yeah, it really would have." Garrett laughed and I joined him. I was glad to see him looking more relaxed than he had been a few moments before. I pulled my jacket on as I stepped closer to him. I had to look up since he was taller than me.

"Seriously though, are you okay? You've been acting strange lately and I'm starting to worry. You know you can talk to me about anything, right?"

"Yeah, I know, Akio. Nothing's wrong though and I'm fine. I've just had some things on my mind, but it's nothing to worry about, I promise," he assured me. I tilted my head and studied his face for any signs of distress, but the smile that spread across his face let me know that whatever was on his mind wasn't something bad.

"Alright, I believe you, but promise me that you'll tell me if you need anything," I demanded, poking my finger into his chest.

"I promise," Garrett said with a chuckle. I felt him stiffen slightly when I threw my arms around him and pulled him in for a hug, but seconds later his arms wrapped around me as he hugged me back. Landon was my best friend, but I had a history with the three men in my apartment and there wasn't anything I wouldn't do for them.

Throughout college, the four of us had seen each other through all-night study sessions before exams, crushes on boys, heartaches over those same boys, and more drunken nights than I cared to remember. The fact that we had each shown our vulnerability to the group and no one had walked away had sealed the bond between us. We knew that no matter what was going on in our lives, or where life may lead us, all we had to do was pick up the phone and the others would come running. It was hard to find that kind of loyalty in the world and I didn't think any of us took that for granted.

"Are you two about finished with your love fest because Jasper and I would like to get to the club sometime tonight. Some of us want to get laid, you know," Travis teased from the doorway.

"Shut up, asshole," Garrett said pulling away from me, but there was no heat in his words.

"I don't think you have anything to worry about," I told Travis as we filed out of my room. "Have you ever left a night at the clubs without getting laid?"

Travis tilted his head and scratched his chin as if he were giving my question a lot of thought. "There was one night a few months ago when Jasper had too much to drink and I had to go with him to make sure he made it home okay," he responded.

"Yeah, but have you forgotten what happened after you tucked me into bed?" Jasper asked with a frown.

"Oh yeah! What was your neighbor's name?" A slow grin spread across Travis's face.

"Tony," Jasper answered darkly.

"Tony, that's right." Travis snapped his fingers. "His mouth was fantastic. He had this thing he did where…"

"Stop right there," Jasper demanded, covering Travis's mouth with his hand. "I can't believe you hooked up with him, I have to live across from the guy. He still asks about you every time I see him. It's awkward as hell!" Travis batted his hand away with a laugh.

"I can't help it that I leave a lasting impression on the guys I fuck." We all groaned at Travis's cocky attitude, but the truth was, we knew he could back it up. Travis had always oozed confidence and sexual prowess. Picking up guys was as easy as breathing for him and I think we were all a bit in awe of him.

"Well, next time leave your *impression* somewhere other than where I live, okay?" Jasper warned.

"Fine," Travis pouted and we all laughed. I waited for them to step out of my apartment before shutting and locking the door behind us.

"God, that was fantastic! I feel so relaxed after the way you three worked me over," Travis suddenly said in a loud voice. "And you, with your tongue," he said as he swept Jasper into his arms and tilted his head up, pressing his lips firmly to our other friend's mouth. My eyes widened in shock, but then narrowed when I realized he was putting on a show for Mrs. Stevenson who was spying on us through her doorway.

"Okay, Romeo. That's enough for one night," I growled as I pulled Jasper away from him. Jasper still looked bewildered and a little uncomfortable as we stepped outside into the chilly night air.

"Apparently, Travis likes to make things awkward with everyone's neighbors," I explained. I could see the understanding dawn in Jasper's eyes.

"Mrs. Stevenson?" he asked. I nodded in answer. He turned and slapped Travis on the chest. "Don't ever do that again. It was like kissing my brother," he said, disgust clearly written on his face.

"Aww, boo, don't be mad. I was just having a little fun. Besides, you should be proud, your lips are so soft and that metal ring is a real turn on." Jasper let out a growl, but I could see the humor in his eyes.

"Too bad you'll never find out how it feels on other parts of the body," he said saucily.

"Damn, I need to find a guy with a lip ring tonight," Travis muttered.

"Don't forget the tongue piercing. It can drive a man wild," Jasper said, sticking his tongue out at Travis, the metal rod through his tongue glinting from the streetlights above. Travis's jaw dropped and his eyes widened. It wasn't often that one of us was able to leave the man speechless and Jasper smiled proudly as Garrett and I each took turns high-fiving him.

I flagged down a cab and we all piled in. Minutes later we were standing in line outside of Lush-Us as the bouncer checked IDs. As I neared the front of the line, I saw that the bouncer was my friend Jakob. I hadn't seen him in several weeks and I was glad to see him back at work. A thought occurred to me as I stepped closer to Jakob and I grinned at him before leaning forward to whisper in his ear.

CHAPTER
Four

Morgan

T HE SMOOTH VOICES OF LITTLE BIG TOWN FLOATED THROUGH the speakers as they sang about having a girl crush. Growing up in the hills of Tennessee, I'd been raised with an appreciation for bluegrass, but I preferred country music. A lot of people thought that country music was all about beer and trucks or cheating, but some of the coolest stories had been told through country music.

The song ended just as I saw Akio's car turn into the lot. I ignored the way my heart sped up as he pulled his car alongside my truck. I was surprised at how excited I was to see him again, given that I barely knew him. I turned the key and pulled it from the ignition before sliding out from behind the wheel. I could hear the thumping bass of some hip-hop song blaring through his speakers before he shut the car off and climbed out.

"Hi!" he said cheerfully over the roof of his car. He wore a pair of stylish sunglasses and the freckles across his nose were even more prominent in the sunlight. His full lips pulled up into a smile and I saw a flash of white teeth. He really was a stunning man.

"Hey! How've you been?" I asked, wearing a smile of my own.

"I'm good. Excited to get this project started." He gestured to the large building. I opened my mouth to respond, but the sound of another vehicle approaching drew our attention. "That's Matt. He could only spare an hour away from the center, but he really wanted to walk through the plans with us one more time before you start working," Akio explained.

"That's great. Like you said on the phone, everything will run smoother if we're all on the same page from the start," I said and Akio nodded his head in agreement.

We watched as Matt pulled up in his Jeep and parked on the other side of Akio. A younger guy climbed out of the passenger seat and I recognized him as the man I'd met when I'd first gone into Agape House. I remembered him introducing himself as Isaac. It had been a very shrewd decision on Matt's part to place Isaac at the front desk. He struck me as a very calm, gentle, and caring person and it probably put the teens at ease to have his face be the first one they saw as they arrived. Matt had described for me just a few of the situations that would send teens their way and the horrors some of them had been through made me physically ill. The pain that humans could inflict on others, sometimes within their own families, was mind-boggling to me and I was thankful once again for the loving family I'd been blessed to be a part of.

After talking with Matt and having him show me around to see what his work was doing for the kids of Chicago, I'd been more determined than ever to make this project my own and to give the kids the kind of place they deserved. I was also extremely proud of my family and their friends for the volunteer work they'd done throughout the years to help keep the place running. I had the greatest respect for them for wanting to expand and improve the center.

"Hey, Isaac! I didn't know you were coming. It's good to see you," Akio said, hugging the man.

"I asked Matt if he'd mind if I saw the plans too. I promise to stay out of the way," he said quietly, fidgeting with his hands.

"You won't be in the way at all," Akio rushed to assure him. "We're glad to have you here to give us your opinions. I know how much Agape House means to you and you'll be able to give us some great insight if there's anything we need to change."

"See, I told you they wouldn't mind you being here. We need your input," Matt told Isaac gently as he rounded the front of his car. I watched as the young man blushed so hard that his ears turned red and he smiled up at Matt. It was obvious that Matt's opinion meant a great deal to Isaac, but Matt seemed unaware of the impact his words carried as he looked up at the large warehouse and then back at me.

"Oh, I'm sorry. Matt, this is Morgan Greene. Morgan, this is Matt –."

"We've met before, but it's a pleasure seeing you again," Matt said. I could sense the surprise and curiosity emanating off of Akio as Matt and I shook hands.

"It's great to see you again, Mr. –," I told him.

"I told you last time just to call me Matt," he scolded with a smile.

"It's great to see you, Matt," I said with a smile. "Would you like to go inside so I can show you where I plan on putting everything?"

"Yes, please. I can't wait to see everything you have planned. I'm terrible at trying to visualize it off of a blueprint, I need to see the actual space," Matt told me.

"I understand. I used to be the same way until I started working with blueprints all the time," I said.

We started moving towards the warehouse, but Akio stopped me when he placed a hand on my arm. Just like the first time we touched, I felt a tremor through the thin layer of my t-shirt where his hand pressed against me. He jerked away as if he'd felt it too and my eyes darted to his. He'd slid his sunglasses on top of his head while he'd been talking with Matt and Isaac so I was able to see the warm chocolate color of his eyes, their depths locking me in place.

"When did you meet Matt?" he asked curiously.

"Before I drew up my plans and placed my bid," I stated simply. Akio narrowed his eyes at me and I knew he wanted more of an explanation. "I like to meet the person I'll be working for, get a feel for who they are and what they're about. In this case, I wanted to know more about the kids that would benefit from a project of this size."

"And?" Akio pressed.

"The strength of those kids is inspiring and the work Matt is doing for them, providing them with a safe place to go and a fresh start at life," I shrugged my shoulders, not sure how to put it into words. "It's amazing and I decided that whether my bid was chosen or not, I wanted to be a part of it." Something passed over Akio's gaze and I wasn't sure what he was thinking, but he simply nodded before turning and heading into the building without another word.

I followed him, admiring the tight fit of his pants as he walked ahead of me. He was dressed in black jeans, black work boots that looked brand new, and a light blue polo shirt that looked beautiful against his skin. There was no denying that I thought Akio was sexy as hell with his tight little body, soulful eyes, and full lips. I quickly adjusted myself in my jeans before the others could catch onto the fact that I was sporting wood as we began our walk-through. I certainly didn't need to start the project off on the wrong foot with the men I was working for.

I spent the next half hour showing them around the building and describing what each bit of space would be used for and what the finished product would look like. Both Matt and Isaac seemed very pleased by the time they got ready to leave.

"You've done an incredible job with the use of space, I don't think even an inch will be wasted," Matt exclaimed.

"I can't wait to see the kids' faces when they walk in here for the first time. This is going to mean so much to them," Isaac added with a happy smile on his face. I smiled too, glad that they approved of the plans and thought they would work well for the center's needs.

"Let us know if there's anything you need from us. Anything at all," Matt offered, sticking his hand out for me to shake.

Akio followed them out to the parking lot while I locked the door and I waved goodbye to them as they pulled away. Akio turned to face me then and I could feel the sudden shift in atmosphere. It was like there was an arc of electricity flowing between the two of us, connecting us together whenever we were near each other. Having the other men there had helped to distract me from its intensity, but it was always present.

I could only imagine how explosive it would be if I ever got him underneath me...or over me as he rode my cock. Akio's gaze turned molten as if I had spoken my thoughts out loud and I watched, transfixed as he swallowed, his throat bobbing in the most tantalizing way. He cleared his throat and my eyes darted to his.

"Are you ready to go?" I stared at him blankly as I tried to remember where we were supposed to be going. A sexy smirk lifted the corner of his mouth. "We need to get you set up on the line of credit at the home improvement warehouse," he reminded me.

"Yeah, sure. Of course," I said, still trying to clear my head. "Do you mind if we take my truck? I need to pick up a few things while we're there."

"Fine by me," Akio answered, using the key fob to lock his car and then circling around to the other side of my truck and climbing up into it.

He snapped his seatbelt as I started the engine and then we were off. Sitting side by side in the cab of my truck, I was suddenly surrounded by the fresh scent of his aftershave and something that reminded me of suntan lotion and I drew in a deep breath, enjoying the intoxicating mixture. Akio pointed out places of interest as we drove through the city, acting as my tour guide.

"Have you always lived in the city?" I asked.

"No, actually, I grew up in a little subdivision. My parents thought it would be safer to raise me outside of the city limits. Still, they wanted me to have the best of everything so we lived outside of the city, but close enough that we could drive into it and spend the day taking in a play or visiting the art or history museums. They'd take me to the local parks so I could run and play." Akio chuckled. "Come to think of it, we spent more time in the city than at home so they might as well have raised me there."

"Do you have any sisters or brothers?" My eyes shot back and forth between the road and his face and I wished I could just pull over so I could study his expressions as we talked.

"Nope, just me. My parents decided when they were first married that they didn't want children." I looked over at him and he must have caught the question in my eyes. "Don't worry," he said, holding a hand up in a placating gesture. "It wasn't like that. I might not have been planned, but that didn't mean they didn't tell me every day what a blessing I was to them. Trust me, I know how much I'm loved by my parents."

"That's good," I said, feeling my shoulders relax.

The next few minutes were spent with Akio directing me to the store since I'd never been there before. We went inside the warehouse which was set up pretty much like any other home improvement store and went to the customer service desk where a friendly woman was waiting to help us. It didn't take long to get my name added to the line of credit and I was given a card that I could scan whenever I needed to make a purchase for the project.

The amount of credit available was staggering, but I remembered that they weren't your average business owners I was working for. Working for Lachlan Edwards had placed me smack dab in the big leagues. Not to mention, Carter and his bandmates, but it was harder for me to see Carter as someone famous. To me, he would always be my bratty little cousin that annoyed the hell out of me and Landon. I loved him to death, but he and Caleb had been little shits when they were younger.

I'd spent some time making a list of supplies that I would need to get started, and after looking it over, the woman assured me that they had nearly everything in stock. My order would be delivered to the job site first thing the next morning and everything else would arrive within two days after that. I thanked her and then headed towards the front door. I felt bad because it had taken longer than I thought and I knew that Akio had to have been bored out of his mind.

"Wait!" he said. I turned around to see what he needed. "I thought you said you had stuff you wanted to get while we were here."

"That's okay, I've taken up enough of your day. I can come back another time now that I know where the place is."

"Don't be ridiculous. There's no reason to make a separate trip when we're already here. I wasn't planning on going into the office today since I knew we were meeting with Matt and then coming here so I have time if you want to go ahead and pick up the things you need," he insisted.

I must have taken too long to respond because he let out a huff as he pivoted on his heel and headed to the corner of the store where the shopping carts were kept. He struggled to yank one free of the chain of carts, finally realizing that he needed to pull up on the one in front of it to release it from its hold. I fought a grin as he returned to where I stood, but the frown he wore told me I had failed.

"Just shut it," he said and I barked out a laugh. "I don't normally shop in places that require a cart," he said, sticking his nose in the air which only caused me to laugh harder.

"What about the grocery store?" I countered.

"Okay, so I use them there, but that's it. Besides, those are normal-sized carts. Why do they have to have such big-ass carts here?" Akio complained. I thought he was fucking adorable when he was being grumpy, but I liked my balls where they were so I kept my thoughts to myself.

"Because they sell big-ass items here," I said instead.

"I prefer firm, round asses myself." He gave a playful wink as he handed the cart over to me and we began making our way down an aisle.

"Kind of like your own?" I shot back, grinning when his steps faltered. Bantering with Akio was quickly becoming my favorite pastime.

"Oh, honey, nobody has an ass like mine," he drawled before taking off in front of me, adding a purposeful sway to his step. I knew he was joking, but I had to agree. His ass was small, tight, and looked like it would fit in my palms perfectly. I pulled my shopping list from the back pocket of my jeans to distract myself from the direction my thoughts were headed and began marking items off as I filled the cart.

"What is all of this stuff for?" Akio asked as we walked down the third aisle. I looked at him, trying to see if he was bored, but all I saw was genuine interest in his face.

"I like to build things in my spare time," I told him.

"You mean like picture frames or something?" he asked.

"No, more like furniture," I explained.

"Seriously? What kind of things have you made?" He sounded excited.

I shrugged my shoulders. "I've made cabinets, rocking chairs, tables. Basically, whatever I feel like at the time. It's just a hobby of mine."

"That's amazing. I'd love to see your work," he exclaimed.

"Maybe I'll show you someday," I said quietly. My workshop was my sanctuary. The one place where I could shut out the rest of the world and just be myself. Someone would have to be very special for me to let them in there. The thought occurred to me that I'd never let David into my old workshop even though we had shared a home. That alone should've told me he wasn't the one, but I'd ignored all the signs.

I finished my shopping quickly after that and paid for my stuff before heading out and loading the bed of my truck. Neither of us spoke for several minutes as we drove back through the city and I was surprised at how comfortable it felt. I'd had fun with Akio, but there also wasn't the need to fill the silence like there often was with other people.

"You mentioned before that you volunteered at Agape House. How long have you been doing that?" I wasn't sure why I was so curious about the man, but there was something about him that intrigued me and I found myself wanting to know more.

"I've been volunteering there for several years now. Landon got me involved when we became friends and I fell in love with the place and what they're doing there. It's hard not to, you know?" he answered.

"Makes sense," I told him. "After just one visit, I'm already thinking about ways I could help out."

"You should. They always need extra hands and you have a lot of skills you could offer."

"What do you do there?" I asked.

"Lots of things. I tutor the kids after school, I help them fill out applications for work and practice questioning them before they go on job interviews. I'm pretty much up for anything they need," he explained.

I listened as he told me about some of the kids he'd gotten very close to as well as the ones he worried about. As he talked, I realized that there was a lot more to Akio Forrest than I'd realized. If you spent any time with him at all, it was clear that he was considerate, caring, and highly intelligent. *How in the world has he not been snatched up already?*

"I feel like I've been doing all the talking. Tell me about you. You grew up in Tennessee, right?" Akio asked, pulling me from my thoughts.

I nodded my head. "Born and raised in the same small town all my life. Our house was an old barn that someone had converted into a home. We had ten acres with a creek to play in and plenty of trees to climb," I told him.

"Yeah, I heard you were quite the daredevil," Akio said with a laugh.

"Oh, that's right, you were asking about me." I arched my eyebrow as I glanced at him. I already knew he'd been asking Landon about me, but I couldn't resist teasing him. His skin turned a pretty shade of pink as he realized he'd been caught, but he quickly recovered, rolling his eyes and turning to look out his side window.

"I spoke to Landon about you, but Landon doesn't spread gossip so I think it's safe to assume that you would only know this if you had been asking about me as well. Am I right?" I could hear the challenge in his voice and it made me smile.

"Yes, your assumptions are correct. I found out that you two had talked about me after I began asking about you," I admitted. Akio turned his head in my direction and I took my eyes off the road long enough to meet his gaze. He looked shocked by my honesty.

"Why were you asking about me?"

"Why did you want to know about me?" We both said at the same time. We chuckled and then I spoke. "You first."

Akio was quiet for several minutes and I began to wonder if he was going to answer the question at all. It wasn't until I pulled into the parking lot where he'd left his car and turned off the engine that he finally spoke. I twisted in my seat, giving him my full attention and I could see the vulnerability in his eyes. Maybe it was just because I was looking so closely, but behind the designer clothes and the camp attitude that he projected to the world, I caught a glimpse of the gentler side he kept hidden. Akio was obviously a proud man and I doubted that many people were able to rattle him, but for whatever reason, I made him nervous and damn it if that didn't make me happy because just maybe it meant I wasn't the only one feeling completely unbalanced when we were together. He cleared his throat as he turned to face me too.

"I asked Landon about you because it made sense to get to know the man I'd be working with over the next few months," he answered simply. I arched a brow at him, challenging him to continue. Akio rolled his eyes in that adorable way that told me I was annoying him and blew out a breath. "Fine, I was curious about a man who could be so sure I would hire him before I'd even met with any other contractors. You were very cocky in that first meeting and I wanted to know why. Your turn," he demanded.

"Okay, your attitude intrigued me, I found your intelligence captivating and I thought you were sexy as hell. Of course, I wanted to know more. I still do." Akio's eyes widened at my admission. I'd always been a very honest person. I spoke my mind and appreciated when others did the same, but in this case, I may have gone too far. I held my breath as I waited for his response. The air in the truck was thick as the electricity that seemed to always be present between us gained strength.

"I may have been attracted to you when we first met too," he said quietly.

"And now?" I pressed. Like magnets being drawn together, we had begun leaning in towards each other until there was barely any space between us. His tongue darted out to wet his bottom lip and I followed the movement with my eyes, wanting nothing more than to discover what he tasted like.

"Now, I think I'd better go," he said. It wasn't until he began to back away that I realized what he'd said.

"Wait!" I said as he opened his door and turned to get out. "I can't tonight, but could I take you out sometime?"

"That depends," Akio said, looking at me over his shoulder.

"On what?" I asked.

"On how my date tonight turns out," he said with a wink. He had shut the door and was climbing behind the wheel of his car before I could respond. I knew he had said it in a teasing manner, but fuck if it didn't piss me off to think of him spending time with another man. The question was, why?

CHAPTER
Five

Akio

CURTIS HAD SOUNDED NERVOUS ON THE PHONE SO I suggested that we ride together to the restaurant so he wouldn't have to arrive alone. He picked me up at six on the dot and I told him how handsome he looked in his khaki pants and white dress shirt. We'd agreed to dinner and a movie, that way if either of us ended up having nothing in common with our dates then we wouldn't have to make conversation during the movie.

Curtis offered to drive and I suspected it was to give him something to do with his hands. I'd never seen him so nervous and as much as I'd been dreading the evening, I was glad that I had agreed to help him out. He was a really nice guy and a good friend. I hoped that he and Jakob would be able to hit it off because he deserved to be happy.

As for my date, I wasn't harboring any expectations. It wasn't that I didn't trust Curtis to choose a nice guy for me, it was just that I was very particular with my taste in men. I usually went for tall, dark and handsome with just a touch of scruff along his jaw, bright sea-green eyes and…I forced myself to stop right there as I realized I'd been picturing Morgan Greene in my head.

It was obvious that there was a lot of chemistry between us and I'd been surprised at how much fun I'd had with him. When he'd asked me for a date, I'd wanted to say yes immediately, but I decided to play it cool instead. With as cocky as he'd been at our first meeting, he deserved to wait for what he wanted. I couldn't very well let him think he was going to get everything he asked for. At least that's what I had told myself and at the time, it had made sense, but afterwards I'd wanted to kick myself. *What if he loses interest and never asks again? What if he meets someone else while I'm off on this unfortunate double date?* I sighed heavily at the thought. What was done was done and I was just going to have to deal with the outcome. Besides, Curtis needed this and I was determined to see it through.

"You okay, buddy?" I asked him as he pulled into a parking space and shut off the car.

"Yeah, sorry. I'm not usually this nervous about dating, but I lost some of my confidence after that guy never called. I still don't get it. We seemed to really hit it off, but I guess I was reading more into it than there was," he said with a shrug. I hated seeing him so miserable and I was more determined than ever to make this night go as smoothly as possible for him. Jakob was a good-looking guy with a great sense of humor and I was confident that even if they weren't a match, they would at least become friends.

"Trust me, if he couldn't see what a great guy you are, then he doesn't deserve to be with you anyway," I told him.

"Thanks, Akio. And thanks for agreeing to this double date tonight. I know you probably have a bunch of other stuff you'd rather be doing, but I appreciate you being here for me," he said sincerely.

"I don't mind at all. Now, what do you say we get in there before our dates think we've stood them up and leave," I joked. Curtis chuckled and I was happy to see him looking more relaxed. We checked our phones as we reached the front door. "It looks like your date is here already. He got us a table in the back," I said as we walked inside.

"Yours just pulled into the lot." Curtis looked up from his phone with a smile. I was glad to see him finally looking excited about the evening. "Why don't you go on in and find the table and I'll wait for your date to come in," he suggested. After telling him the last name to ask for, I made my way to the hostess stand.

"I'm here for the Gregory party," I informed the young woman behind the stand who smiled at me like there was nothing in the world she would like more than to help me find my seat. She scanned the list of names in front of her and then looked up at me with her radiant grin still in place.

"Right this way, sir. It looks like we're still waiting on two members of your party."

"Yes, they're here. They'll be inside in just a few minutes," I explained.

"That's wonderful," she exclaimed cheerily.

Jakob smiled as I walked towards him and I saw his eyes dart over my shoulder. I took the seat directly across from him, leaving room for Curtis to sit in the seat next to him once he and my date joined us.

"Don't worry, he's coming. He was waiting for my date to park his car," I told him. I saw Jakob's shoulders relax.

"Oh, good! I was afraid for a minute that this was all just your way of getting me to go out with you. I like you as a friend, but you're not my type, Akio," he said seriously.

I felt my jaw go slack as shock hit me. I tried to form a response, but my brain seemed to have quit working. I'd known Jakob for several years and never in all that time had I looked at him as more than a friend. Besides, I certainly didn't need to trick anyone into dating me. I felt myself getting angry and I had just decided to give him a piece of my mind when I noticed the way his shoulders were shaking and the smile he was trying to fight back.

"You asshole," I hissed. Jakob lost the battle at that point and erupted into a fit of laughter.

"Oh boy, I wish you could've seen your face. That was priceless," he said, gasping for air.

"I'm glad I could be here for your amusement. Are you about finished?" I said dryly, crossing my arms over my chest.

"I'm sorry, I couldn't resist the opportunity to mess with you," he said, finally getting himself under control.

"That's okay, I'll get even eventually," I promised. Jakob's eyes twinkled with mischief and he opened his mouth to respond, but was interrupted by a man's voice.

"Jakob?" My head swiveled to Curtis who was staring down at the man across from me with a mixture of disbelief and was that pain? My eyes darted back to Jakob who was looking at Curtis. Shock and regret seemed to be the prominent emotions etched on his face. It was obvious that the two of them already knew each other, but I wondered what had happened to cause such a serious reaction from each of them.

Jakob pulled himself together first and he quickly stood, grabbing Curtis by the elbow and steering him in the direction of the restrooms. It wasn't until they'd walked away that I noticed the man who had been standing quietly behind Curtis during the confusing exchange. I wasn't sure which one of us was more surprised as I stared into the beautiful sea-green eyes of Morgan Greene.

"What are you doing here?" I asked. My head was spinning with how quickly the mood of the evening had changed, not to mention the fact that Morgan was right there in front of me.

"Curtis and Caleb coerced me into going on a double date when I stopped by Romero's for dinner the other night," he said with a scowl. "They thought I needed to get out and meet people."

"You don't seem very happy about that," I said, suddenly feeling disappointed. His face smoothed out as he met my gaze.

"The coercion part, no. How it's turned out so far, yes." His lips lifted into a small smile and I felt something stir in my gut. "Do you mind if I sit down?" He gestured to the seat next to me.

"Oh no, sorry. I forgot my manners with everything that just happened," I said. Morgan sat down, his elbow brushing against mine and my pulse sped up at his close proximity.

"So, do you know what that was about?" Morgan tilted his head in the direction Curtis and Jakob had taken.

"No clue. I didn't even know they knew each other. Given their reactions, I'd say it probably wasn't a good idea on my part to set them up," I said as I cast a worried glance towards the bathroom where my friends had disappeared to.

"Like you said, you didn't know. Whatever issues they have between them, has nothing to do with you and it isn't your fault," Morgan assured me. "Besides, the fact that they're still in there and no one has had to call the police yet gives me hope that they're working it out."

"Thanks," I said with a chuckle. I appreciated him adding some levity to the situation. "This really sucks though because I've always prided myself on my matchmaking skills. I've got a perfect record," I stated proudly.

His smile grew, eyes crinkling at the corners and I thought to myself what a beautiful man he was. The more time I spent with him, the more obvious it became what a genuinely nice guy he was which wasn't all that surprising, considering he was a Greene. Every member of the Greene family was kind, warm, and accepting. I had often wished that there were more people in the world like them. I was lucky to have them as friends.

Although, if I was being completely honest with myself, the feelings I had whenever Morgan was around, went well beyond the boundaries of friendship. I had a sneaking suspicion that he felt the same way about me, especially given his admission earlier that he'd thought I was sexy when we first met. I'd had to fight the urge to grab him and devour his mouth when he'd told me that. His expression turned serious and his gaze dropped to my lips as we sat there, as if he'd just read my thoughts.

We were so caught up in each other, we didn't notice Curtis and Jakob approaching the table until they sat down across from us. I turned towards my friends and was relieved to see them both smiling. Their lips looked suspiciously red and swollen which told me they'd been doing more than just talking in the bathroom.

"I take it you two worked things out?" I teased, giving them a knowing look. Curtis turned a bright shade of pink and Jakob chuckled as he looked over at him adoringly.

"Yeah, we did," Jakob answered. I was dying to know what had happened, but I didn't want to be rude and come right out and ask. Luckily, Curtis knew I would be dying of curiosity and he didn't make me suffer for long.

"You remember the guy I told you about?" he asked.

"You mean the one that you liked a lot?" I answered with a question of my own.

"You said you liked me?" Jakob's entire face lit up as he turned to face Curtis.

"Wait a minute, that was you?" I narrowed my eyes at Jakob. "Why didn't you ever call him like you said you would?" I demanded, jumping to Curtis's defense.

"I wanted to, trust me," Jakob said, holding his hands up in a defensive manner. "I got a call the next day that my mom had been in a car accident and suffered a broken leg. She lives in Wyoming and didn't have anyone else to take care of her so I flew there to help out.

I dropped my phone at the airport and broke it. When I went to get it replaced, I ended up losing all my contacts."

"So that's why I didn't see you at the club for a long time," I said in understanding.

"Exactly. I was gone a couple of months and by the time I got back, I figured that even if I had Curtis's number, he probably had already forgotten about me. I mean, if I couldn't stop thinking about him after one night, surely someone else would've snatched him up by then," Jakob said quietly. My heart went out to him. He had to have been going crazy thinking that he'd missed out on an opportunity with a great guy. Curtis reached over and took Jakob's hand on top of the table.

"I was too hung up on you to even think about anyone else," he admitted. "I only agreed to this double date because Akio needed a wingman." I felt my eyes bug out of my head, but I kept quiet when Curtis winked at me. I knew he was trying to assure Jakob that he hadn't been moving on.

"Well, I'm glad everything worked out," I said, smiling at each of them. "Things are worked out, aren't they?"

"Yeah, things are good." Curtis grinned shyly.

We were all still smiling when the waiter came to take our orders. We quickly scanned the menus that we'd ignored in all the excitement and gave him our selections. He left to get our drinks and we settled into a nice conversation. Curtis and Jakob were excited to hear about Morgan's plans for Agape House and offered to help with the fundraising.

We continued getting to know one another over dinner and I was surprised at how easily we all got along. There was none of the stilted conversations or awkward silences that were often present on a first date. Jakob regaled us with funny and sometimes horrifying stories of his job as a club bouncer, Curtis told us about his trip to Europe the previous summer where he studied under some of the same chefs that had taught Caleb.

I could feel Morgan's eyes on me throughout dinner and I smiled as he pulled my chair out for me when it was time to leave. The cinema was just a few blocks away and the weather was nice, so we all agreed to leave our cars at the restaurant and walk there instead. I insisted on paying for our movie tickets and popcorn since Morgan had bought my dinner. He frowned at the suggestion, but nodded his head when he saw how serious I was.

The movie we'd chosen had been out for several weeks so there was no one else in the theater which was fine with me. I hated sitting in a crowded theater. There was always that one person who wanted to talk over the movie, spoiling the experience for everyone else. I sat down between Morgan and Curtis with Jakob on the other side of him.

We settled into our seats as the lights lowered and the trailers began for upcoming movies. My breath hitched and I felt the blood rush to my cock as Morgan's long fingers reached between my legs to get a handful of popcorn from the tub I had placed there. My eyes moved in his direction and I saw him wink at me through the light on the screen. He knew exactly what he was doing to me, fucker.

Two can play at that game. I reached for my own handful and ate it then I made a production of licking the butter from the palm of my hand and sucking it slowly off of each finger. I heard Morgan moan beside me and the sound sent a tingle that travelled from the base of my skull, down my spine and straight to my groin. I started to turn towards him, but a louder groan pulled my attention in the opposite direction.

My eyes widened when I saw Curtis and Jakob making out beside me. They were completely lost in each other as their mouths fused together and their hands roamed over each other's bodies. When I heard the sound of a zipper lowering, I turned to Morgan who was also watching the live show with a huge grin.

"Come on, let's give them some privacy," he whispered in my ear. I glanced back at my friends, not sure if I should leave them without saying anything, but then I caught the movement of Jakob's arm and I knew that he'd found his intended target inside of Curtis's pants. Without another word, Morgan and I stood and quickly filed out of the row of seats. It wasn't until we made it out into the lobby area of the theater that we lost it.

"I wonder how long it'll be before they realize we left?" I said around my laughter. I tossed the rest of the popcorn into a trash can as we walked out of the theater.

"I'm not sure they'll even notice when the movie ends."

Morgan reached down and took my hand in his, threading our fingers together. My eyes shot down to our joined hands and then back up at his face. He continued walking as if holding my hand was the most natural thing in the world to him. I couldn't remember the last time a man had held my hand and I found myself smiling as I moved along beside him. We walked in comfortable silence, taking our time as the city continued to rush all around us.

"Oh shit," I exclaimed as we entered the restaurant parking lot. "I forgot that I rode here with Curtis. I'll order a car," I said, pulling my phone out of my pocket and opening the app. Morgan covered my phone with his hand.

"Don't be ridiculous. I'll take you home, my truck is right over there," he said pointing across the lot.

"Are you sure?" I asked. I hated to make him go out of his way.

"I'm your date for the evening and I'm going to make sure you get home safely," he said, sounding almost offended that I would think otherwise. I smiled at his gallant attitude. I didn't know if it was from being raised in a small town or just who he was, but Morgan Greene had a charm about him that I hadn't run into a lot with the guys I'd dated. He made me feel important, special. I shoved my phone back into my pocket as I followed him to his truck and I quirked a brow at him when he opened my door for me.

"Really going all out tonight, aren't you? You think all this chivalry is going to earn you a kiss at the end of the night?" I teased as I climbed into the truck. I sucked in a breath as Morgan reached for the seatbelt and fastened it over my lap. His face was just inches from mine and I could feel his breath on my cheek as he spoke.

"I'm chivalrous because you deserve to be treated properly," he said, his deep voice reverberating through my chest. I shivered as his thumb smoothed over my bottom lip. "As for the chance to kiss these lips, well, I'd never say no to that."

Morgan's eyes met mine and then he pulled away, shut the door, and circled the front of his truck before I remembered to breathe again. My cock pressed painfully against my zipper and my heart beat wildly in my chest. The man was smooth, no doubt about it.

We made small talk on the way to my apartment, only stopping when I needed to give directions. Morgan described what it was like, growing up in Tennessee and I smiled at the fondness in his voice as he talked about his family. He was obviously very close with his parents, same as me. As we talked, I discovered that we had several things in common. We both loved Mexican food, action movies, and going to the beach, although Morgan liked to surf while I preferred to watch hot guys and work on my tan.

We had a lot of differences too. I spent most of my free time reading, going dancing, and hanging out with my friends. Morgan on the other hand, was an adventurer. I listened raptly as he described his experiences bungee jumping, skydiving, and rock climbing. I was in awe of him, but at the same time I felt a little sick at the thought of him throwing himself out of a plane and hurtling towards the ground.

"I'm sorry things were so awkward with Jakob and Curtis tonight," I said, trying to change the subject.

"Don't be, they were both very nice. I'm glad they were able to talk things out and move past their misunderstanding," he replied.

"Yeah, me too and hey! At least my matchmaking record is still intact," I joked as we pulled up alongside my apartment.

"Maybe Curtis's are as well," Morgan replied as he put the truck in park and turned to face me. I looked at him in surprise, and the gentle look in his eyes as he stared back at me, filled my chest with warmth.

"It's funny, I was dreading this date just a few hours ago and now, I couldn't be happier with how it turned out," he said.

"It's been a good night. Even if we didn't get to watch the movie," I chuckled.

"I wasn't paying attention to the movie anyway." I watched as his eyes turned a darker shade of green and I knew he was remembering the way I had teased him by sucking on my fingers. My pulse picked up speed and my cock began to plump in response to the way he was looking at me. He leaned towards me and I felt myself moving in the same direction.

"Earlier you said you wanted to see how your date went tonight before you agreed to go out with me. Not very nice by the way." He smirked. "So, what's the verdict?"

"I think I'll need that kiss before I can decide for sure." My voice sounded shaky as I answered.

Before I'd even finished speaking, Morgan had wrapped a hand around the back of my neck and drew me towards him. Our eyes were open as he pressed his lips to mine, as if neither one of us wanted to miss a single moment of our first kiss. His lips were soft, but firm as he took control and I soon opened up to him, letting his tongue dip inside.

I sighed into his mouth as our tongues began dancing and swirling around each other, perfectly in sync, as if they'd always known each other. My hands went to either side of his head and my fingers gripped his soft hair, holding him to me so he couldn't retreat. Eventually, we were forced to break apart for air, but still close enough for our breaths to mingle.

Our gazes remained locked on each other, watching the surprise and the lust and the wonder we were feeling, play out in the other's eyes. We hadn't known each other all that long, but there was definitely something happening between us. Whether it was simply lust or something more, I had no idea, but I was eager to explore it further.

"Would you like to come upstairs?"

CHAPTER
Six

Morgan

I PRESSED AGAINST AKIO, MY HANDS ON EITHER SIDE OF HIS waist. I nuzzled my face in the crook of his neck as he fumbled with his keys, trying to unlock the door to his apartment. His smooth skin and the scent of him were battling to see which one would drive me insane first. He tilted his head to the side, granting me better access and let out the most adorable mewling sound as my teeth grazed over his pulse point.

He was so responsive to me and it made me feel powerful and protective all at once. It had been so long since I'd felt that kind of connection with another man. *Hell, has it ever been like this before?* Not that I could recall and certainly not with David. I forced myself to push thoughts of my ex aside. The man had taken enough from me and I refused to let him be any part of what was about to happen.

I lifted my head and turned to look behind me at the sound of a door creaking open. My eyes narrowed when I caught sight of two eyes staring at me through the crack of the opened door. Akio must have felt my tension because he turned and peered over my shoulder. I wouldn't have heard his frustrated groan if I hadn't been standing so close to him.

"Hi, Mrs. Stevenson!" he said with false cheeriness. "It's a beautiful night out, wouldn't you agree?" My eyes darted back and forth between Akio and the open door, but there was no response. "Okay then, we're just going to go inside. Have a great night." I was surprised when he turned back around as if the exchange was the most natural thing in the world. He slid his keys in the lock, that time getting the door open.

Following him inside, I scanned the tiny apartment. The door opened up into the living room which was decorated in shades of black and gray, with splashes of color thrown in through strategically placed accent pillows and a soft looking blanket, folded neatly over the back of the couch which separated the living room from the kitchen. There were several pieces of artwork on the walls and a few framed pictures of family and friends sitting around the room.

The kitchen walls were painted the same gray as the living room with crisp white cabinets and countertops. A hallway led off to the left where I assumed the bedroom was. Akio's home was modern and well organized, but instead of being cold and untouchable, it gave off a feeling of vibrancy and life. Not all that different from the man who lived there, the man who was standing much too far away if you asked me.

"Would you like something to drink?" he asked, setting his keys down in a bowl on the table by the door.

"No, I'm not thirsty, thanks." I was expecting him to be shy now that we were alone in his apartment, but I should've known Akio would surprise me. He stalked forward until he was standing directly in front of me. Our height difference was made more apparent when he had to lean up on his toes to wrap his arms around my neck.

"Where were we?" he teased. I chuckled, leaning down so he wouldn't have to strain to reach my mouth.

As our lips met, we melted into each other in a way that felt much more familiar than it should've, considering that was only our second kiss. It was as if my body already knew his, but everything was still new and exciting in all the best ways.

I nibbled at his bottom lip, tugging on it gently with my teeth and he moaned in my arms. My tongue swept into his mouth, tasting and exploring. A tremor went through my body as his hands roamed up and down my back. As our kiss deepened, I pulled him forward by the hips so that his groin was nestled against my own and we both groaned as our cocks lined up through the fabric of our clothes.

We ground against each other as passion ignited between us and my excitement turned into desperate need. I wanted to feel his velvety skin sliding against mine and to taste every single inch of him. I wanted to know his hidden secrets and what he looked like when he came. I wanted to know everything I could about the man that had me twisted up in knots.

I reached between us and ran my hands over his shirt. He stopped kissing me and pulled back so he could look at me. He saw the question in my eyes and answered with a single nod. I cupped his face in my hands, bending down for a gentle kiss and then I began unbuttoning his shirt, slowly revealing the smooth, flawless skin that was hidden underneath.

Akio tugged at the bottom of my shirt, pulling it free from where it was tucked into my pants then he slid it up and over my head in one deft move. I ran my hands over his bare chest as he worked his arms free of his shirt, reveling in the feel of all that silky skin beneath my fingertips. The urge to taste him was too great so I bent down, taking one nipple into my mouth and sucked hard, swirling over it with my tongue and teasing it with my teeth until it stood at attention.

Akio fisted his hands in my hair and cried out. I moved to give the other nipple the same attention as my hands got busy unfastening his pants and sliding down the zipper. I could feel his lips in my hair and then his hot breath in my ear.

"You're driving me crazy," he whispered and I felt my cock soaking my briefs with pre-cum at the sound of his strained voice.

I dropped to my knees in front of him and looked up into his beautiful brown eyes as I slid his pants down his legs. His lips were soft and wet from my kisses, his jaw was pink from rubbing against my stubble and damn if that didn't make me all kinds of happy to see my mark on him. He kicked his shoes and pants off to the side and I let my eyes roam over him. I loved his tight little body, the sleek muscles under velvety skin, his slender waist, and the thin line of dark hair that disappeared into his underwear.

My mouth watered at the sight of his sexy, red boxer briefs and I leaned in to nuzzle my face against the silky material, running my nose up and down over his bulge and breathing in the clean musky scent of him. My hands smoothed a path up the sides of his legs, running around the back of him and cupping the firm globes of his ass before grabbing his boxers by the waistband and sliding them off.

Pre-cum leaked from the tip of his cock as it bobbed up and down in front of my face and I couldn't resist leaning forward to capture the liquid on my tongue. I moaned at the salty, sweet flavor of him. I grasped the base of his dick and swirled my tongue over the tip before tilting my head to the side and running the flat of my tongue up and down the veins there. His cock was long and slender and I sucked on the tip, jerking my hand up and down the length of him, and sucking on the head until I was rewarded with another burst of salty goodness.

Akio fisted his hands in my hair and I could tell he was trying to hold back so he wouldn't choke me so I grabbed onto his ass and pulled him forward, taking him all the way down my throat over and over until he began thrusting his hips with abandon. My dick demanded attention, having been left out of the fun for too long, so

I opened my pants as quickly as possible and freed it from its constraints. I moaned around my mouthful of Akio's cock as I took my own in hand and began working it up and down.

After several more minutes of that, I had to stop, squeezing the base roughly to hold off my release. If this ended up being my one time with Akio, I wanted to make it last as long as possible. I could tell that he was getting close too, so I pulled back reluctantly, letting him slide out of my mouth. A sexy little growl sounded from the back of his throat, letting me know that he wasn't happy that I had stopped, but then I heard his breath falter as I stood and divested myself of the rest of my clothes.

He bit his lip as his eyes travelled over my body slowly. I stood there, letting him look his fill. *How long has it been since anyone had looked at me with so much appreciation and hunger in their eyes?* The answer was simple. Too long.

"You're so sexy," Akio whispered and I sucked in a breath as he stood on his tiptoes and traced my lips with his tongue.

I opened for him and my knees grew weak as he began sucking on my tongue. He reached between us and I thought I would lose my mind when his hand closed around my aching shaft, jerking his hand up and down its length a few times and twisting his wrist when he reached the tip. *How can he possibly know how much I love that?*

Akio looked down between us as his thumb swirled over the head of my cock, coating it with pre-cum and then pressing down into my slit. He lifted his head and looked directly in my eyes, giving me a teasing wink as he pulled his thumb back up in front of his mouth and swiped it with his tongue. He let out a loud moan and his eyes fluttered closed as he tasted me for the first time.

"Fuck!" I growled, losing the tenuous hold I had on my control. I reached my arms around him and grasped his ass in my hands, lifting him up in the air. He laughed in surprise as he wrapped his legs tightly around my waist and threw his arms around my neck.

"Aren't you just full of surprises," Akio exclaimed, smiling widely.

"You have no idea," I rasped.

"Then show me," was his response.

The look on his face turned molten and he leaned forward, capturing my mouth with his as I carried him out of the living room in search of his bedroom. My head began to swim as we kissed, but my need for him at that moment was stronger than my need for air. He shook his head as we passed the first door so I continued on to the only other door. I swung it open and moved forward until my knees hit the end of the bed. I slowly lowered him and we both gasped in a lungful of air as he released his tight hold on me.

Akio was still breathing heavy as he slid up the bed with a serious expression and I crawled on my hands and knees, following his every move, like a predator. When he reached the pillows, he crossed his arms and raised them above his head in complete surrender. A tremor shook my body as I gazed down at the offering before me. I had never seen anyone more exquisite in my life and he was mine to enjoy, at least for that one night, and I planned on enjoying him over and over again.

I lay down on my stomach, settling myself between his splayed legs and wrapped my lips around his hard cock. His body arched up off the bed as I sucked him all the way down, not stopping until my nose was pressed against his neatly trimmed hair. I held there for a few seconds, loving the feel of his cock in my throat before I slid off, leaving a trail of saliva between his dick and my lips.

Not giving him any time to think, I dove back onto him, bobbing my head up and down his shaft. For several minutes, the only sounds in the room were of Akio's guttural moans and the wet slurping sounds of me sucking him. I felt him get even harder in my throat and I pulled off with a wet pop.

"No, no, no. Please don't stop," he begged.

"Don't worry, I'm going to take good care of you, baby," I promised.

I slid my hands under his thighs and pressed on them until he raised his knees to his chest, locking his arms underneath to hold them up and exposing himself to me. My mouth watered at the sight of his perfect, pink hole. I flattened my tongue and swiped it from the base of his crack all the way up to his sac. I took a moment to pay some attention to his balls, sucking one and then the other into my mouth and swirling my tongue around them.

I looked up the length of his body and saw that Akio was staring down at me, pure desire written across his face. I kept my eyes locked on his as I stuck two fingers into my mouth and wet them then I lowered my head and ran my tongue around his rim.

"Oh, God!" Hearing his cries only served to increase my need so I pressed my face between his legs and began feasting on him. I licked and sucked at his entrance, pressing a wet finger inside and gently working him open. He was tight, but his body responded to me beautifully and soon, I had him relaxed enough that I knew I wouldn't hurt him.

I moved up onto my knees and Akio twisted his body to the side, reaching into the bedside table drawer and pulling out a bottle of lube and a condom and tossing them to me. He studied me under heavy lids, running his hand up and down his cock as I slid the condom on and then poured some of the lube onto the palm of my hand. I slicked myself and then applied a liberal amount to his hole. I wasn't exactly small and I didn't want to cause him any unnecessary pain.

Akio slid one of the pillows under his hips and pulled his knees to his chest as I lined my cock up with his opening. I was trembling with the need to be inside him, but I forced myself to hold steady as I looked down at him.

"Are you ready?" I asked, not recognizing the husky sound of my voice. He was quiet for a couple of heartbeats and I held my breath, worried that he'd changed his mind.

"I'm ready," he whispered.

I watched his face for any signs of distress as I slid inside, slowly breaching the ring of muscles that wanted to fight against my entry.

I reached for his cock and began stroking it as I gave him time to adjust to my girth. Soon, I felt him relax and we both breathed a sigh of relief as I slid the rest of the way in. His tight heat enveloped my shaft and my body ached with the need to move, but still, I waited for him.

"I'm good," Akio said and I began to rock my hips back and forth in a slow, even motion. His smooth walls gripped me tightly, stealing my breath with every glide in and out. He brushed my hand aside and began stroking his own cock.

"I'm not going to break. Now, fuck me like you mean it," he demanded, the challenge clear in his eyes. My movements faltered for just a second and then I felt a smile spread across my face.

"Okay then, Mr. Bossy," I teased.

"You have no idea," he said, throwing my earlier words back at me. I couldn't help the laugh that burst from my chest and Akio smiled up at me, looking very pleased with himself.

Determined to give him exactly what he'd asked for, I slid out of him and flipped him onto his stomach. He huffed out a surprised laugh, but then moved up onto his knees with his head down on the mattress and wiggled his ass at me, taunting me. I cupped his firm butt cheeks in my hand, kneading them with my fingers and then with the flick of my wrist, swatted his right one with the palm of my hand.

His laughter turned into a moan and I watched as his skin pinked up into the perfect shape of a handprint. He thrust his hips into the pillow below, obviously as turned on by what I'd done as I was. I licked my way up his spine, tasting his sweat until I reached his ear. I nibbled at his lobe and he moaned again, writhing under me.

"You like it when I spank you?" I growled in his ear.

"Yes! Yes, I need more. Please," he pleaded desperately.

I lifted up and knelt behind him and he stilled, waiting for it. I paused several seconds, letting the anticipation grow and then landed a series of three smacks, all in quick succession to his left cheek before moving to the right and delivering two more.

"Please, please, please," he chanted, his voice slurring as if he were drunk. I grabbed his hips and pulled him up further onto his knees and then plunged my cock back into him. My fingers dug into his hips as I began moving in and out of his tight depths with long, powerful thrusts. Akio pushed himself up, tossing the pillow aside and bracing himself with one hand on the mattress and one flat against the headboard as I rocked his body back and forth.

"Morgan!" he shouted as I hit his prostate. The sound of my name on his lips had me right on the jagged edge, but I refused to go over unless he went with me. Without slowing my movements, I let go with one hand and swatted his ass, first one side and then the other.

Akio screamed at the same time his ass clamped down on my cock. He body vibrated with his orgasm and after two more thrusts, I joined him. Lights swirled behind my eyelids and my body went rigid as the most powerful orgasm I'd ever had in my life held me in its grasp. There was nothing I could do but ride out the wave as long as I could.

Akio collapsed underneath me and I followed, trying my best not to crush him with my weight. I might have blacked out for a second or two because the next thing I knew, I was lying beside him and he was lying on his stomach, his head turned towards me, with a look of wonder on his face.

"You okay?" I whispered.

"I'm better than okay. That was..." He trailed off as if searching for the right word.

"Incredible," I supplied.

"I was going to say amazing, but incredible works too," he said with a sleepy smile, his eyes growing heavy.

"Hey! You can't go to sleep yet," I told him. He glanced down at my dick which was still sheathed in the condom and growing soft.

"You're good, but even *you* need a little recovery time there, mister," he teased.

"Haha!" I retorted. "I meant that we should clean up and change the sheets and then I want to put some lotion on your butt so you don't get too sore."

I smoothed my hand gently over the abused skin, feeling the heat from where I'd spanked him and I hoped I hadn't gone too far. I'd never tried that with anyone else before and I wasn't even sure what had possessed me to try it with Akio. It had been a risky move on my part because he could've easily gotten mad and asked me to leave. He must have noticed the worry on my face because he reached down and grabbed my wrist in his hand.

"I'm fine." I stared into his eyes, searching for any regrets he may have. He sighed. "You are the only person who hasn't treated me like I'm made of glass. You treated me like a man, like your equal and I appreciate that so much, so please don't take that away by worrying that you hurt me. I would have told you if it was too much, okay?"

"Okay," I agreed. I could see how much it had meant to him and I felt proud that I was able to give him something that no one else had, but at the same time, I could see a deeper sadness in his eyes that I wanted to get to the bottom of. I knew better than to push him though so I changed the subject. "Can I ask you a question?"

"I think we know each other well enough for one question," he joked. I smiled at him, loving the easy way we got along with each other.

"Have you ever done that before?"

"Done what exactly? Because I hate to burst your bubble, big guy, but I wasn't a virgin," he said with a smirk.

"Not that, smartass," I said with a chuckle. "I meant the spanking. Have you ever done that before?"

"No. I mean, I've read about it and watched it on porn before, but I never thought it would be something I'd like," he answered honestly.

"And did you? Like it, I mean." His eyes widened as he looked at me like he was trying to decide if I was serious or not.

"In case all the screaming and the hands-free orgasm weren't enough of an indication, yes, I loved it," he said sarcastically.

"Oh, well good," I mumbled, feeling embarrassed by my need for reassurance. Akio tilted his head to the side as he looked at me. I wanted to squirm under his watchful gaze, afraid that he would see too much, see all of my failures.

"I loved everything we just did," he answered sincerely, all trace of teasing gone.

I felt myself relax into the sheets, not even realizing how tense I'd gotten. I hated that I was suddenly feeling so unsure of myself. I wanted to enjoy whatever time I had left with Akio, so that was what I was going to do.

"Take a shower with me?" I climbed from the bed, tossing the condom into the trash can and holding out a hand to him.

"Fine, but only because it looks like you're recovering quite nicely and I want to see what other tricks you have up your proverbial sleeve," he said with a wink as he climbed from the bed and started to sweep past me.

I threw an arm around his waist before he could get too far and pulled him to me. He was laughing as I leaned down and sealed my mouth over his. I felt him sway in my arms and I wrapped my arms securely around him, holding him steady. After a few minutes, I let him go and was pleased to see his pupils blown wide. He turned on wobbly legs and I watched him saunter out of the room, a smile spreading across my face. Being with him was refreshing and fun. My last thought before I ran after him to join him in the shower was that one night with Akio was not going to be nearly enough.

CHAPTER
Seven

Akio

"IT'S OPEN," I SAID DISTRACTEDLY AS SOMEONE KNOCKED ON the door. I continued working, only pulling my eyes away from my computer screen when I heard Landon's voice.

"Hey! You busy?" he asked as he strode into my office.

"Yes, but I could really use a break," I told him. I had been poring over spreadsheets for the last three hours and my head was starting to throb, not to mention the pain in my back from sitting still for so long. I leaned back in my chair and stretched as Landon sat down on the other side of my desk.

"I'm surprised to see you here. I figured you'd be buried under all of the last-minute wedding preparations," I told him.

"Micah and I haven't had much to do, actually. Mom, Emma, and Michelle have pretty much taken over everything." He rolled his eyes as he said it, but I knew he wasn't really upset.

"You love that your mom and sisters are taking care of things. You know they'll put together the perfect wedding for the two of you and besides, with them handling the details, it gives you more time alone with that sexy fiancé of yours," I replied with a knowing grin.

"I'm glad that they're so excited about our wedding and having fun with the planning and believe me, I do appreciate everything they've done, but they call constantly with questions…often at the worst possible times," Landon explained with a groan.

"Oh, that's not good," I chuckled.

"It's not, not at all. Nobody wants their sex life interrupted by their mother calling with a question about flowers or their sister calling about centerpieces or their other sister calling to ask what to have engraved on the napkins," he said in exasperation.

"Hold up, they're having the napkins engraved? I didn't even know…" I trailed off when I saw the hard look Landon was giving me.

"Not the point," he hissed and then glared as a laugh escaped from me.

"You know, you could just not answer the phone, right?" I suggested.

"I've tried that!" he cried, throwing his hands up in the air. "Mom's not as bad, but if it's my sisters and they can't get ahold of me, then they start calling Micah's phone. When that doesn't work, they alternate between his phone and my phone every couple of minutes. Then they show up at our house and ring the bell over and over again until we finally answer." I couldn't help but laugh.

"Do you think they know what they're interrupting?" I asked.

"Oh, they definitely know and that's exactly why they're doing it. Notice how they never call during the day when I'm at work, it's always when they know Micah and I are at home together," he pointed out.

"Wow! I'm suddenly very grateful to be an only child," I teased.

"Well, you are welcome to mine anytime you'd like," he joked back. The truth was that I would've loved to have the kind of relationship that Landon had with his siblings and despite his grumblings, I knew that he adored every one of his sisters and brothers. They were a very close group and while they had fun picking on one another, there wasn't anything they wouldn't do for each other.

"If it makes you feel any better, you'll be on your honeymoon next week and then they can't bother you," I reminded him.

"I can't wait. Two full weeks at a remote cabin in the mountains of Northern Georgia. No phones, no television, no people for miles. Nothing but me and Micah and the great outdoors," he said with a smile.

"Okay, the uninterrupted time with your man I get, especially given how busy the two of you always are, but being cut off from everything? No way. What are you even supposed to eat? It's not like you'll be able to call for Chinese to be delivered." I shuddered at the thought. Landon laughed at what I'm sure was a horrified expression on my face.

"Don't worry, we'll stop at a store along the way and stock up on food," he assured me with a chuckle. "Micah loves hiking and fishing and I grew up doing all that with Morgan when we would go to Tennessee."

Landon continued talking about the outdoorsy things he and Micah wanted to do over their vacation, but my mind got snagged on the sound of Morgan's name and drifted off to thoughts of our night together. Goose bumps broke out over my skin at the memory of his body pressed to mine, skin against skin. He'd taken me two other times that night, each one, somehow, getting better than the time before. I'd loved how insatiable he'd been, as if he couldn't get enough of me, *but he would* I'd reminded myself. I knew he would because everyone did, eventually.

The sound of Landon snapping his fingers in front of my face drew my attention and the amused expression on his face had me wondering how long I'd been lost in my own thoughts. I felt my face heat at the thought of Landon knowing exactly what I'd been thinking about. He tilted his head at me and his eyes narrowed.

"I really lost you there. Thinking of anyone in particular?" He was smiling, but I still heard warning bells going off in my head.

"Why would you assume I was thinking about a person? I might have been thinking about the work I was doing before you interrupted me," I said, hating the defensiveness of my tone, but unable to stop it.

"Oh, I don't know. Maybe because I lost your attention about the same time I mentioned my cousin. Or it could be because I talked to Carter who talked to Caleb who talked to Curtis. When exactly were you going to tell me about your double date?" he asked. My shoulders slumped in resignation when I saw the devious smile he wore. There was no way he was going to let me get away with not answering his question.

I explained how the date even came about, from being suckered into it by Marco and Curtis to being completely surprised to find that Curtis had fixed me up with Morgan. I then told him about Curtis and Jakob having known each other already and about the misunderstanding between them. Landon laughed as I told him about Curtis and Jakob's very heated make out session in the movie theater and how Morgan and I had slipped out to give them some privacy. I did not mention however, the fact that his cousin and I had gone on to spend the night together. I figured there were some things that were better left unsaid.

"So, did you two hit it off? Do you think you'll see each other again?" he asked enthusiastically.

"Yes, we will definitely be seeing each other again; every time I visit the job site," I deadpanned. The excited look on his face melted off as he glared at me.

"You know that wasn't what I meant," he said, rolling his eyes at me.

"I know, I'm just not sure how to answer that," I told him honestly.

"Would you like to see him again?" Landon asked gently.

"I'm not sure it matters what I want," I said.

"What the hell does that mean?" Landon's voice rang out, but he quickly lowered it as I glanced towards the door. "Did Morgan do or say something to make you feel like your opinion doesn't matter?" he asked angrily.

I sat there for a few seconds just staring at him. Morgan was Landon's cousin, his favorite cousin and yet he was ready to jump to my defense if he thought Morgan had hurt me in some way. I knew that if the situation were reversed, he'd be upset with me for hurting Morgan, but the fact that he didn't just automatically side with his cousin meant the world to me. That's why Landon was my best friend, even though I'd known Travis, Jasper, and Garrett much longer. Landon was one of the very best people I knew and his loyalty to me and others that he cared about was an attribute that was very hard to find in most people and one that I was grateful for every day.

"No, it was nothing like that. Morgan was a perfect gentleman throughout the date." I watched as Landon visibly relaxed.

"Then what did you mean?" he pressed.

"You know how guys in the past have always seen me. They think I'm too high-maintenance just because I like nice clothes and care about my appearance, or they look at my size and see me as some delicate little flower that needs protection. They all think I'm fun at first, but then they walk away once they get to know me and see that I have a mind of my own and I'm not afraid to speak it." I shrugged my shoulders as if it didn't bother me what those guys thought, but Landon knew otherwise. He'd seen me get hurt time and time again by someone I thought was going to stick around and actually get to know me, but instead disappeared after just a couple of weeks.

"Trust me, Akio, the right guy is going to come along someday and he's going to find all of those things endearing. You're an amazing man and you deserve to find someone who sees that all those qualities you just named, aren't things to be avoided, but rather are the things that made you into the incredible person you are. Who knows if Morgan is that man, but either way, there *is* a guy out there who's perfect for you." The look on Landon's face was so sincere that I had no doubt that he'd meant every word. I just wished that I could believe that what he was saying would really happen.

"Thanks, Landon. I really appreciate that and I hope that you're right." His forehead scrunched up and I knew he wanted to say more, but I stood, making a production of looking at my watch. "I need to get going. I wanted to stop by the job site and see how things are going on my way home." It took me a moment to realize why Landon's face suddenly brightened, but then it hit me.

"Hold your horses, Cupid. I'm not going there to see Morgan specifically, I'm simply doing my job." Landon opened his mouth to say something, but I cut him off. "Besides, don't you have things you need to finish up so you can go home and answer more pertinent wedding questions instead of getting laid?" I teased.

"Don't remind me," he groaned and I laughed at the dejected look on his face. He stood as I gathered my things and logged off my computer then he walked me out of my office and to the front of the building. I turned and faced him before I walked out.

"You guys are heading to Tennessee in the morning, right?" I asked.

"Yes. We wanted to get there early so we didn't feel so rushed and we could get settled in before the rest of the family invades the cabin," he joked.

Landon had told me about the huge cabin that his family owned. It sounded wonderful from everything he'd told me, but he had a very large family so I knew he wasn't joking about them invading. From the sounds of it, there would be no empty rooms in the cabin once everyone arrived and several family members had chosen to stay at a nearby hotel just as I was doing.

"Well, have a safe trip and I'll see you in a couple of days."

"You be safe travelling too. Text me when you get there so we can meet up," he said. We hugged each other and then I stepped out into the sunshine. I was halfway to my car when I heard him call out. "Tell Morgan that his favorite cousin said hello!" I turned around, walking backwards.

"Okay, if you think that's what Caleb would want me to say," I joked. Landon looked up and down the street to see who might be around and then flipped his finger up in the air. I was still laughing as I climbed into my car and started the engine.

My stomach was in knots on the drive over to the job site. It had been a little over a week since I'd seen Morgan, not since the night of our double date and I was nervous about facing him. We'd exchanged a few texts here and there since then, but we'd both been swamped with work.

The team that Landon had put together to help him organize the worldwide tour for Carter's Creed had done an outstanding job, but it was his first time taking on a huge project such as that without having my input and so he'd asked me to go over everything with him in great detail to make sure they hadn't forgotten anything.

As it turned out, the team had double booked the band on two separate occasions and forgotten to set up the flights between the U.S. and England. While those may seem like huge problems to have overlooked, they were actually quite easy mistakes to make given the magnitude of the planning involved for such an event. It took us many days and a lot of compromising on the part of the venue operators and ticket sellers, but we eventually got it all straightened out and Landon felt much better about leaving on his honeymoon.

Morgan, on the other hand, had been busy hiring the last of

his crew and beginning the daunting task of knocking down walls, tearing out windows, and clearing away the years of debris left behind when the manufacturer had abandoned the old warehouse that would be made into the new Agape House. He'd mentioned a few times in his texts how tired he was and I worried that he wasn't getting enough sleep. Then I'd stop myself when I'd remember that he was a grown man and didn't need me worrying about him. After all, it wasn't like he was mine.

I repeated that fact to myself many times over the last week, almost like a mantra. Despite the way he'd smiled at me the morning after our night together or the way he'd kissed me goodbye, almost as if he were reluctant to do so, I knew that I had a tendency for getting ahead of myself when it came to guys and I always ended up disappointed.

I couldn't stop my thoughts from turning to Morgan in the days since, a couple happening at the most inopportune times. On those occasions, I was grateful that I had a desk between Landon and myself so he wouldn't notice the effect my thoughts were having on me. The longer I went without seeing him though, the more I began to question whether or not the connection I'd felt with him that night had been real or imagined. I'd vowed to take whatever happened between Morgan and myself one day at a time and to be cautious with my heart, the same heart that began to beat wildly in my chest as I pulled into the parking lot of the warehouse.

There were several trucks and a few cars in the lot and as I turned off my car, I could hear the distinct sound of hammers pounding and something that sounded like a drill or a saw running inside the old building. Workers moved about and someone sang loudly and very off-key to a song playing on the radio. The place was alive with activity, but it seemed to be an organized chaos which I could appreciate.

I climbed from my car and slid my keys into my pocket as my eyes scanned the premises, searching for Morgan. I finally found him and my stomach did a little flip. He was dressed for the job in jeans, work boots, and a gray t-shirt that stretched tightly across his broad chest. He reached up and scratched the scruff along his jaw and my mouth watered.

He was with two other men and they had their heads bent as they went over a blueprint that had been spread over the hood of his truck. Morgan ran a finger over the lines of the drawing as he explained something to them and a chill rushed over my body at the memory of that same finger trailing a path down my spine.

As if he'd heard my thoughts, Morgan's head shot up and his eyes met mine. A smile spread across his face and I smiled back, releasing the breath I hadn't realized I'd been holding. He said something to the two men and they glanced over at me before rolling up the blueprint and walking back into the building. Morgan walked towards me and I admired his swagger as I moved towards him as well.

"Hey there! I didn't know you were coming here today." He peered down at me with those mesmerizing green eyes and I nearly forgot how to speak.

"I wanted to see how things were going with the renovation. I've been meaning to stop by, but we've been really busy at work and it's been dark before I've gotten out of there," I explained, relieved when my voice came out sounding normal.

"I'm glad you're here. Come on, I'll show you what we've done so far." I walked beside him, trying not to read too much into the fact that he'd said he was glad I was there or the fact that he sounded like he really meant it.

Morgan stopped at his truck and reached across the seat for something, coming back with a bright yellow hard hat. He grabbed another one off the hood of the truck and placed it on his head then held the first one out towards me. I stared at it stupidly, not sure what he wanted me to do with it.

"Everyone has to wear one of these inside the building," he explained and my breath caught in my throat as he stepped forward and placed it on top of my head. My eyes scanned the area, wondering if anyone had noticed the way he'd smoothed the wayward strand of hair out of my eyes.

"I probably look ridiculous," I informed him, convinced I resembled a child playing dress-up.

"You could never look ridiculous. Besides, it's about keeping you safe, not how you look," he said before leaning down to whisper in my ear. "Just so you know, I'm picturing you wearing nothing but that hat and a toolbelt and it is sexy as fuck." My eyes were wide and my skin felt hot as he winked at me then turned at the sound of someone calling his name.

He told me to go ahead and have a look around while he spoke to his crew member so I headed into the building without him. Once my eyes adjusted to the lack of sunlight, I scanned the interior and what I saw was nothing short of amazing. Not only had the entire place been swept clean and unnecessary walls been taken down, but it looked like they were actually ahead of schedule.

New concrete had been poured to replace the cracked and uneven surface of the floors, the windows had been reframed so that once the glass was installed, it would look more like a home than an old factory and I could see that the electrician had been busy updating the wiring that ran throughout the building since what had been there previously was no longer up to code and deemed unsafe for children. Several of the new walls that would make up offices for the various staff members had already been framed in and were just waiting on drywall to be hung.

The building had an old freight elevator, but I didn't trust it, despite Morgan's assurance last time that it was perfectly safe to use, so I chose to take the stairs instead. I wandered around the second floor, checking out all the latest developments and that was where Morgan found me.

"Well, what do you think, Mr. Boss...man?" he asked playfully, eluding to the time he'd called me bossy in bed. I opened my mouth to reply, but cleared my throat instead as a man walked into the room we were in.

"I'm impressed, Morgan. I didn't expect you to be so far along already. It's really coming along quickly and that's a testament to your skills as a leader," I told him.

"Thanks, but let's not get carried away. There are always problems and setbacks that go along with any job, I'm just here to make sure that those problems stay small and don't turn into major catastrophes," he said modestly.

"Well, you promised me you were the man for the job and now that I've seen the quality of your work, I know that you were definitely not all talk." My voice dripped with innuendo, turning the tables on him and I watched, delighted, as Morgan's eyes darkened with lust. He waited patiently for the man to find what he was looking for and leave the room and then he moved quickly, backing me up against a wall and placing his hands on either side of my head, caging me in.

"I haven't been able to stop thinking about you," he whispered, sounding surprised. "When can I see you again?" I felt my body stiffen as my self-doubts bubbled right under the surface of my skin.

"You mean, when can we fuck again?" I snapped, hating the way my voice wavered.

Morgan stared down at me, confusion written clearly across his face. I felt like I had something stuck in my throat and I was suddenly having trouble breathing. I needed to get out of there and far away from him.

"That wasn't what I meant at all. I mean, the sex was…" His eyes grew wide and he blew out a deep breath then grinned at me and I felt myself beginning to relax. "It was unbelievable, but I was actually referring to the date I asked you out on. A date where it's just you and me." I tried to hide my surprise, but the soft look on Morgan's face told me that he'd already seen more than I'd wanted him to.

"Oh, I uh…I'm sorry, I misunderstood," I stammered. My gaze dropped to the floor, but Morgan cupped my chin and lifted my head, forcing me to look at him.

"Make no mistake about it, I loved being with you that way and I would definitely not be opposed to doing that again, but I had fun with you on our double date and I'd like to go out with you again. I want to get to know you better."

I started to answer him, but my words were cut off as he slanted his lips over mine. His tongue swept in, exploring my mouth and filling me with the flavor of spearmint and Morgan. My legs felt shaky as he continued kissing me senseless and I threw my arms around his neck to keep myself from falling. He ended the kiss and we held each other as we tried to slow our heart rates.

"I need to go," I whispered and I felt his shoulders tense under my arms. "I have some things I need to take care of, but call me and we'll set up a time for that date," I promised.

Morgan pulled his head back so that he could see my face and the smile he gave me was nothing short of dazzling. He stepped back without a word and took my hand in his, leading me down the stairs and out of the building. The sun had lowered while we were inside and the building made large shadows across the pavement. He walked me to my car and then opened the door for me.

"Aren't you worried about what your crew might think about you walking around, holding my hand?" I teased. Morgan shook his head.

"I made it clear to every person when they were hired that I was a proud gay man and that the project we would be working on would be for an LGBTQA youth center. I told them that if they had a problem with either one of those things that there were probably plenty of other construction crews that would love to hire them. Only one person got up and left the interview at that point," he said with a shrug. He acted as if it were no big deal and maybe someday it would be, but for now, it was a pretty incredible thing to do.

We said goodbye and then I climbed into my car. Morgan leaned in through the open window and gave me another quick kiss before stepping back so I could leave. I waved out the window as I pulled away and I was halfway home before I realized I was humming the tune that had been playing when he kissed me. I wasn't sure what it was since I never listened to country music so I looked it up as soon as I pulled up outside my apartment building. I smiled when I found it and immediately downloaded it onto my phone. I'd be able to listen to "In Case You Didn't Know" whenever I wanted and remember that kiss, that moment when a man told me that he wanted to get to know me better.

CHAPTER
Eight

Morgan

I TOSSED MY BAGS INTO THE BACK SEAT OF MY TRUCK AND SHUT the door. After one last search inside the house and my workshop to be sure I hadn't left anything on, I climbed into the truck. I checked my phone for any missed calls or texts from the crew and smiled when I saw Akio's name in the list of text messages. I'd texted him after he'd left that night, unable to stop thinking about that kiss or the way he'd clung to me when I'd backed him up against the wall.

His reaction when I asked if I could see him again had surprised me to say the least. He'd acted angry when he asked if I meant that I wanted to fuck him, but I heard the shakiness of his voice and saw the look on his face that I was sure he didn't want me to see. The look was a mixture of hurt, disappointment, and resignation and I wanted to know who had hurt him in his past. Who had made him feel like that was all he was worth? How could anyone spend any time at all with Akio and not see what a funny, intelligent, and caring man he was? I opened up the text thread between us and smiled as I read it for what was probably the hundredth time.

ME: Hey! I was thinking…

AKIO: That sounds dangerous.

ME: Funny guy. You should do standup.

AKIO: Nah, I'm holding out for the lead role in a movie.

ME: Let me guess, a romantic comedy?

AKIO: Hell no. I'd be in a thriller. I want to run down the street screaming at the top of my lungs as some guy wearing a mask chases me with a meat cleaver.

ME: Well, you do have a great scream, if memory serves me correctly.

ME: Hello? AKIO?

AKIO: Sorry, had to pick my jaw up off the floor.

ME: LOL!

AKIO: So, you were thinking…

ME: Oh, that's right. I seem to get easily distracted around you.

AKIO: 😊 😊 😊

ME: You're going to Landon's wedding, right?

AKIO: Of course, he's my best friend.

ME: I assumed you were and I was thinking we should ride together.

AKIO: Oh!

ME: Unless you were bringing a plus one with you…

AKIO: No, nothing like that. I was just surprised.

ME: It makes sense if you think about it. We're going to the same place, we could keep each other company on the way there and we'd save gas. Plus, carpooling is good for the environment.

ME: Do it for the environment.

AKIO: Ok. But only for the environment. 😉

ME: You're a good man, Akio Forrest. Pick you up Thursday

after work?

AKIO: Sounds good.

I closed the message and placed my phone in the cup holder. I checked the rearview mirror as I turned the truck around in my driveway and caught the excited look in my eyes. I was looking forward to going home, seeing my family, and celebrating Landon and Micah's wedding, but it was the eight hours of uninterrupted time with Akio on the way there that I was looking forward to the most.

That surprised me because after the way things ended with David, I thought I would need some time before I'd be ready to even entertain the thought of getting close to another man. The thing was, I hadn't counted on Akio coming into my life or the way he'd make me feel. If I had to describe the feeling in one word, it would be *happy*, which was something I hadn't felt in a very long time.

He was sitting on the bottom step outside his building when I pulled up, three suitcases at his feet. I got out and quickly went around to help him with his bags. I grabbed two of them and he followed me with the other, placing them alongside mine in the back seat.

"You do know we're only going for a few days, right?" I teased.

"You don't think all of this happens by accident, do you?" he replied sassily, brushing his hands down his body. My eyes followed, taking in the black, button-fly jeans that fit him perfectly, the gray long-sleeved shirt that looked really soft, and the darker gray sweater he had thrown over his shoulders. He looked perfect.

"Three bags it is then," I said agreeably. I heard his chuckle as I shut the door and then rushed to open the passenger door for him.

"Thank you," he said quietly as he brushed past me to climb inside.

We made small talk as we left the city. He asked how my day had been and I listened as he told me about the various musicians he'd met while working. Some I'd never heard of, but a few surprised me because their names were always in the news and splashed across the covers of the magazines in the checkout lane. Akio laughed when he saw the stunned expression on my face, reminding me that I was related to one of the most famous musicians of our time. That shocked me even more because I never thought of Carter as being famous. He was just Carter.

We decided to drive through rather than stopping for dinner since we were already going to arrive in Tennessee in the middle of the night. We'd agreed the night before that it would be best to leave after work and have the rest of the night to sleep instead of leaving in the morning and getting there just in time for the festivities. Neither one of us wanted to be too tired to enjoy the weekend with our closest friends and family.

"Everything alright?" I asked when Akio pulled his phone out of his pocket as we waited in line for our food.

"Oh yeah, I just need to confirm my reservation at the hotel," he answered distractedly.

"Why are you staying at a hotel?" I demanded. Akio looked up from his phone, surprised by my reaction.

"Because the cabin was going to be completely filled up with your family members. It's no big deal. I already talked to Landon about it and he told me about a nice hotel that's not too far from the cabin," he explained calmly.

"No, absolutely not. There's no reason for you to stay in a hotel when you can stay with me at my parents' house," I insisted. Akio's mouth dropped open at my suggestion, but he didn't have time to respond because the teenager who'd taken our order picked that exact moment to bring our food to the window. I handed the sack of food to Akio, who was still regarding me strangely and then pulled away from the restaurant. We were about a mile down the road before he spoke.

"You want me to stay at your parents' place? With you?" he asked hoarsely.

"Well, we don't have to do it that way, but they might wonder why a stranger was staying with them while their son's at a hotel," I joked. I glanced at him out of the corner of my eye and burst out laughing when I saw the evil look he was giving me. "Oh, come on, that was funny." Akio rolled his eyes and shook his head at me, but I saw the twitching of his lips before he turned away.

"Won't your parents think it's a little strange that you're bringing home some random guy?" he asked as he began handing out the food.

"You're not just a random guy," I said a little sharper than I'd intended and he turned his head to stare at me. "You're Landon's best friend and I'd like to think you and I are friends as well so that makes you more than just some random guy," I explained.

"Still, they have no idea I'm coming and we'll get there in the middle of the night. I'd feel bad showing up unannounced like that. I'll just stay at the hotel," he stated as if it were final. I popped a fry in my mouth and then pressed a button on the steering wheel. A woman's robotic voice sounded through the Bluetooth system asking me what I wanted.

"Call Mom," I instructed her.

"What are you doing?" Akio hissed, a look of panic on his face. I held my index finger up to tell him to wait a second.

"Hey, honey! Are you on your way? Your dad and I were just talking about you. Hang on a second and I'll put you on speaker so he can talk too." I smiled at the sound of my mother's voice. It was typical of her to talk a mile a minute. My dad and I had learned a long time ago to just let her finish whatever it was she was going on about before we tried to jump in. A second later, Dad joined her on the line.

"Morgan? Are you doing okay?" he asked.

"Yeah, I'm doing great. The traffic wasn't too bad leaving the city so we're making really good time. We should be there around one or two depending on how many stops we make along the way," I told them.

"We? Is one of your cousins with you because I know Landon's already here. His fiancé is so sweet and *handsome*! We met him earlier today and I'm just so happy for them. They said..." I shook my head as I cut her off.

"Mom! Hang on a second. I've got you on speaker. I have a friend with me, he's actually Landon's best friend and he was going to stay at the hotel in town since there won't be any room at the cabin," I explained. I looked over at Akio who was staring at me. The expression *deer in the headlights* came to mind and I had to fight back a laugh. My parents were both quiet and I held up a hand to Akio, counting down with my fingers, 3...2...1 and then pointed to the speaker.

"Well, that's ridiculous," my mom scoffed, right on cue. "There's no reason for...what's your name, honey?"

"Um, it's Akio. Akio Forrest, ma'am," he answered with an adorable squeak.

"There's no reason for you to stay at a hotel, Akio, when we have more than enough room right here. I'll just fix up the guest room so it's ready for you when you get here," she said.

"No, really. I don't want to be any trouble, ma'am," he insisted.

"Don't be silly. We're happy to have you. Besides, you're keeping Oliver safe on the ride home and we appreciate that more than you could ever know. Now you boys be safe and we'll keep a light on for you."

"Thank you?" Akio said quietly, but it came out as more of a question.

"Oh, and one more thing, Akio. We are very informal people so there's no need for any of that ma'am stuff. Call us by our names, Susan and Jeff, okay?" she informed him.

"Yes, ma'am...er...Susan. Thank you and thank you too, Jeff. I appreciate you letting me stay there," Akio said quickly.

"Bye, guys. I love you," I said.

"Bye, honey, be safe driving. We love you," they both said over each other. I hung up the phone and popped another fry in my mouth with a satisfied grin.

"What the hell just happened?" Akio asked in exasperation.

"You were worried that my parents wouldn't want you to stay at their house. I called them so you could hear directly from them that they would love to have you there. Problem solved," I said happily.

"I could kill you right now," he informed me.

"Okay, but make sure you cancel your hotel reservation first so they don't charge your credit card." I smiled at him innocently. He answered with a low growl and turned to face the window. We finished eating in silence and I wondered if maybe I'd really upset him and he was going to refuse to speak to me the rest of the trip. I was relieved when he spoke up a minute later.

"Your parents seem really nice," he said quietly.

"They're pretty great," I told him.

"Sounds like you guys are close. I like that. I'm close to my parents too." He cleaned up the garbage left over from our dinner and rolled the bag up before setting it on the floor by his feet.

"We are. I'm really lucky to have them as parents. They've always supported me in everything, even with my decision to leave. I know it wasn't easy on them to see their only son move so far from home." I couldn't help the wave of guilt I felt as I pictured their faces as I drove away that last time.

"Why did you move?" he asked.

"It was just something I needed," I replied casually. We had been having a good time and I didn't want to ruin it by explaining about my failed relationship with David. Akio seemed to sense that I didn't want to talk about it and I was grateful when he moved on. That was, until I heard his next question.

"So, Oliver?" I winced. I'd really been hoping he hadn't heard my mother say that.

"Yeah," I said reluctantly.

"Oliver's not a bad middle name. Why do you look like you swallowed a lemon?" he asked with a chuckle.

"It's not my middle name. It's my first name," I answered with a sigh.

I clenched my jaw. I could feel Akio's stare as he puzzled out what it was I wasn't saying. I kept my eyes on the road as I waited for it to dawn on him. It didn't take as long as I hoped before I heard his swift intake of breath, followed by peals of laughter. My shoulders drooped.

"Oh. My. God," he said, wiping tears from his eyes. He sounded just like a character from a show I liked when he said it, but I wasn't finding the situation funny. After all, I'd heard it more times than I could remember.

"Oliver Morgan Greene? Your initials are OMG?" He broke out into another fit of laughter and I tried to stay serious, but there was something contagious about the sound of Akio's laugh. It was a distinct sound that reminded me of summer days, ice cream, and happiness. *I could listen to that sound forever.*

"Alright, funny man. Get it out of your system," I said with a smile.

"I'm sorry. You have a really great name, honestly." He wiped the last of the tears from his cheeks as he calmed down. "The initials all together though…" He shook his head and smiled at me.

"Maybe my parents didn't like me as much as I thought," I mused.

"No, I could hear it in their voices. They're crazy about you."

"They're my parents, they kind of have to like me," I joked.

"Well, I don't have to like you, but I do," he said so quietly I would've missed it if I hadn't been paying close attention. I turned to look at him and my heart leapt inside my chest at the shy smile that he gave me.

"I like you too," I told him, surprising myself with just how *much* I was beginning to like him.

"This is beautiful," Akio said, sitting up in his seat and peering out the front window as I pulled into the long drive that led to my parents' house. We'd continued to make good time and arrived at just a little past one thirty in the morning.

"It looks even better in the daylight. I'll show you around tomorrow," I told him proudly as I parked the truck and turned off the headlights.

I opened my door and smiled at the comforting sounds of tree frogs and owls. We grabbed our luggage from the back seat and I fished my house key from my pocket as we walked up the steps of the deep-set front porch. Mom had left the kitchen light on, as promised, so we didn't have to stumble around in the dark.

I heard a familiar noise coming towards the kitchen and I set our bags down on the floor as I dropped to one knee. Carly, our golden retriever and my childhood playmate, came to welcome me home. She'd been a gift for me on my fifteenth birthday and the two of us had been inseparable. Over the years she'd developed hip problems and could hardly see anymore. I could tell that it was getting harder for her to get around, but right then, she was simply a dog that was happy to see her boy and I was happy to see her too. Her tail wagged cheerfully and I rubbed the top of her head, ducking my head to brush my cheek against her soft fur. I looked up in surprise when Akio dropped to the floor and began petting her.

"What's her name?" he whispered.

"Carly," I told him, laughing quietly as she rolled over so he would give her a belly rub. "I think she likes you."

"She's beautiful. I always wanted a dog, but my dad is allergic," he explained.

"That's too bad. Carly was a great companion when I was growing up. Still are, aren't you, girl?" I cooed at her. She rewarded me by licking my hand. Akio covered his mouth quickly as he yawned.

"Come on, I'll show you where your room is so you can get some rest." I stood quickly and held a hand out to him. His was warm and soft as he slid it into mine and I felt the same tingling right under the surface of my skin that I always felt when we touched. Once he was on his feet, I reluctantly let go so that we could pick up our bags.

I led the way up the stairs to the loft area of the house. I pointed out the bathroom at the end of the hall and then flipped the light on in the guest room and set Akio's bags down at the foot of the bed. The room looked exactly the same as it always had with hardwood floors and white lace curtains and a blue comforter on the bed. It was simple, but comforting and I smiled when I saw that my mom had placed a vase full of flowers on the table by the bed in preparation for Akio's visit.

"We don't have to be anywhere until tomorrow evening so feel free to sleep in as late as you want. My parents will be down at the cabin first thing in the morning I'm sure, so it should stay quiet around here," I told him.

"Okay," he said, glancing around the room nervously.

"My room's right across the hall if you need anything," I said.

He nodded and we stood there just staring at each other for several seconds. I felt that old shift in the atmosphere and I crossed the room in two long strides, gathering him in my arms and covering his lips with mine. His arms curled around my neck and I pulled him tighter to me. The kiss went on for a long time with us taking turns nibbling and tasting each other. He fit so perfectly in my arms as if he'd always belonged there, that when he pulled away, I felt the loss immediately.

"Good night, Morgan," he said softly.

"Sweet dreams, Akio," I whispered back. He smiled softly and I backed out of the room, holding his gaze as I slowly shut the door. I leaned my forehead against the door and blew out a long breath. *I think I might be in trouble.*

CHAPTER
Nine

Akio

I WOKE IN A STRANGE BED IN A ROOM THAT DIDN'T SEEM FAMILIAR at all. My first thought was "Oh hell, what did I do?" but then I remembered the wedding and travelling with Morgan.

Morgan.

Warmth filled my chest as I thought about him and the fun we'd had on the way there. When he'd first asked if I wanted to ride with him to Tennessee, I was worried that we wouldn't be able to come up with enough to talk about and there'd be long spaces filled with awkward silences. What ended up happening however, was quite the opposite. In fact, there was very little time in which we didn't talk and the few quiet moments that did occur were more comfortable than awkward. Being with Morgan was as easy as breathing, yet exhilarating enough to leave me breathless.

My mind wandered to the kiss we'd shared the night before. We'd been staring at each other, neither one of us quite ready to end what had been a rather fun-filled night. Suddenly, he was coming at me, his intentions clear in his eyes and then his lips were on mine. The scruff along his jaw rubbed my face deliciously and sent waves of pleasure running up and down my spine. He'd taken control of the kiss, gently demanding that I open to him. I'd allowed him entry and his tongue had swept in, teasing, exploring, and tantalizing me in a way that made my head spin and my heart feel like it was going to beat its way right out of my chest. The kiss ended far more quickly than I would've liked and before I'd known it, he was saying good night and was out the door.

My hand slid under the covers and pressed against my cock as the memory played out in my mind like a scene from a movie or in this case, the beginning of a very dirty porn video. I reached under the waistband of my sleep pants and wrapped my hand around my aching cock. I moaned loudly and then slapped my other hand over my mouth, my eyes springing open as I remembered where I was. I listened carefully for any sounds outside my door and then breathed a sigh of relief when I didn't hear anything. The last thing I needed was for the first impression I made on Morgan's parents to be of me jerking off to thoughts of their son.

I threw the covers off and climbed out of bed, ignoring the complaints of my dick as he realized he wasn't going to get any relief. Grabbing my toiletry bag, I pulled the door open slowly, peeking through the crack to see if anyone was around. I could hear the faint sound of voices coming from downstairs and I wondered if Morgan's parents were getting ready to head over to help with the wedding preparations.

Morgan's door was shut so I assumed he was still sleeping. Rolling my eyes when I realized I was acting like poor Mrs. Stevenson when she spied on me at home, I stepped out into the hallway and made my way towards the open door of the bathroom. I closed the door behind me and set my bag on the counter then reached in and turned on the shower. I pulled out the items I would need from my bag as I waited for the water to warm up, and then peeled my clothes off and climbed under the spray.

The water felt heavenly as it loosened my stiffened muscles and washed the last of the fogginess from my brain. I washed quickly so that I wouldn't use all the hot water and then got out, dried off, and brushed my teeth. When I was finished with the rest of my morning routine, I wrapped a towel around my waist and grabbed my bag to head back to my room and get dressed.

I yanked the door open and stepped out of the bathroom, but drew to a sudden stop when I noticed Morgan leaning with his shoulder against the wall and his arms crossed. The smirk he'd been wearing disappeared as his eyes travelled down my bare chest and stopped at the towel I was wearing; the towel that was quickly tenting under his heated gaze.

The naked desire I saw on his face had me feeling empowered and I moved closer until I was standing right in front of him. His hair was damp and he smelled like body wash, fresh and clean. I crooked my finger at him and he bent his head down so that my lips could meet his ear.

"That shower felt so good. All that hot water, rushing over my body. The only thing missing, was *you*," I whispered. My tongue darted out to trace the shell of his ear and I felt him shudder before I stepped back.

"I'm here now," he replied and I was thrilled with how strained his voice sounded. Given the fact that he could turn me into a puddle of goo with just a single look, it was only fair that I should be able to tease him occasionally. He reached for my towel and gave it a little tug, but I swatted his hand away with a shake of my head.

"Uh uh, not in your parents' house. You'll just have to wait." Morgan tilted his head and banged it gently against the wall with a frustrated groan and I had to bite my lip to keep from laughing as

I stepped around him and moved towards my room. I opened the door and looked over my shoulder. He turned to watch me so I blew him a kiss and let my towel drop to the floor. I heard his sharp intake of breath right before I shut the door between us. Inside my room, I leaned against the door with a giant smile on my face. *God, that was fun!*

I got dressed quickly. Morgan had been dressed casually so I chose to wear my favorite pair of jeans and a blue V-neck t-shirt that was soft to the touch. The jeans might have been a little tight, but I liked the way my ass looked in them, hence why they were my favorite.

I stood in front of the mirror, making sure my hair was styled perfectly, all except for that wayward clump of hair that constantly fell over my forehead, refusing to be tamed. If it weren't in the front of my head, I swear I'd cut the thing off.

Satisfied with my appearance, I opened the door and smirked when I saw Morgan standing in nearly the exact same spot I'd left him in. He came towards me and put his hands on my hips. I loved how casually he reached for me, as if he couldn't stand to be near me and not be touching me in some way. It made me feel special, like the connection we felt with each other extended beyond the bedroom. I laid my hands on his chest, feeling his heart beating underneath the white t-shirt he had on.

"You're dressed," he pointed out.

"Keen observation skills you've got there, mister. Perhaps you should've been a detective," I teased.

"I liked what you were wearing before," he said, jutting his bottom lip out in an adorable pout.

"Hmm, I don't think I was wearing *anything* the last time I saw you." I tilted my head up, giving him a coy look.

"Exactly," Morgan said in a low voice. His lips brushed gently over mine and I could feel his breath against my face when he spoke. It was hot and smelled minty and my mouth watered with the need to taste him. "Just so you know, I will get even for you teasing me, earlier. Perhaps a spanking is in order." I gasped when his hands slid down and cupped my butt, pulling me up against him roughly. All my blood rushed to my cock, leaving me hard and dizzy. He gave my lips a quick peck and then started to back up. I tried to grasp his shirt in my hands, but he pulled away with a chuckle.

"Mom made food for whenever we got up. You hungry?" he asked easily as if he hadn't just tilted my world on its axis.

"What?" I shook my head trying to keep up with the quick turn of events.

"My mom left food for us to eat," he said slowly, annunciating each word.

"Um, sure. Just give me a minute. I need a minute," I repeated lamely. I closed my eyes, willing my erection to go away. That was twice that morning that my cock had been denied and he was angry. "How the hell do you do it?" I whispered angrily.

"Do what?" he asked innocently.

"Turn me into an incoherent ball of mush every time. Just when I think I've gained the upper hand," I grumbled. I blew out a long, slow breath.

My cock finally settled back down although I was sure he was still holding a grudge, but that was okay because so was I. I refused to have sex in Morgan's parents' home, but I was really beginning to regret not having a hotel room that we could use. I opened my eyes and was surprised to see him staring at me with a soft expression. I searched my mind for what could've put that look on his face and my eyes widened when I recalled my words. I scrambled to think of something to say that would keep him from freaking out, but before I could come up with anything, he reached out and cupped my face in his hands.

"I'm glad to know I have that effect on you, but you are *not* the only one. I can barely think straight when you're around. The way you look, the way you smell, your smile; you drive me wild, Akio." I slid my hands up around his neck and curled my fingers into his soft hair as he lowered his head and kissed me. I backed away though before we could get too carried away, afraid that one more time and my cock would never forgive me.

"Come on. Let's get something to eat." Morgan took my hand as we walked down the steps, giving it a gentle squeeze. I smiled.

After a quick lunch, Morgan showed me around his parents' property. He was right, it was even more beautiful in the daylight. I'd never given much thought to living outside of a city or subdivision, but I had to admit that there was a certain peacefulness that came from being surrounded by nature. I wasn't an outdoorsman in the least, but even I could appreciate the beauty of walking through the woods and hearing all the animals scurrying about or sitting along the lake and watching a mother duck with her little ducklings trailing behind her. I could almost picture Morgan running around there as a young boy and it brought a smile to my face.

Morgan and I had stretched out on the soft grass surrounding his parents' lake. I was using his stomach as a pillow and he was running his fingers through my hair as we stared up at the clouds and talked about anything and everything. The sun was on my face and my head moved up and down each time he breathed in or out and my eyes fluttered closed.

Fingertips glided gently across my eyebrows, down my nose, and traced the outline of my lips. I opened my eyes and tilted my head to look at Morgan. He was smiling down at me, tiny little crinkles forming at the corners of his eyes. His green eyes shone in the sunlight and his skin looked golden and healthy. He was a beautiful man, both inside and out and I knew without a doubt that I was falling for him, hard.

I wanted to ask him what it was we were doing, what he wanted to have happen between us, but I was worried about spoiling the time we were sharing and more than a little afraid of what his answer might be so I kept quiet, deciding to just try to live in the moment and enjoy whatever time I had with him.

"I hated to wake you, you looked so peaceful sleeping there, but we need to get over to the cabin soon," he explained. I lifted my head off him and glanced around, surprised to see the sun had moved behind the trees.

"Sorry I fell asleep on you. How long was I out?" I sat up and stretched, a loud yawn escaping me.

"You obviously needed the rest and you weren't out that long; only about half an hour." Morgan sat up beside me and brushed the grass from my back. "Besides, I was outside on a beautiful day with a gorgeous man using me as his pillow. It doesn't get any better than that."

His words made my heart flutter in my chest and I turned my head to look at him over my shoulder. He met my gaze and smiled at me and I answered with a smile of my own. He stood and holding his hand out, helped me to my feet.

It didn't take long to drive to the Greene's cabin and I was shocked by how big and luxurious it was. When Landon had described his family's cabin, I'd pictured a normal-sized cabin with a few extra rooms for guests. The place in front of me was nothing of the sort. It was about the size of a luxury hotel, but with all the charm and personality one would expect from a home the Greenes owned.

"This is really remarkable," I said as I took in the colorful flower gardens that outlined most of the property and the breathtaking view of the Great Smoky Mountains in the distance. "No wonder Caleb and Landon each wanted to have their weddings here."

"Yeah. When I was a kid, I used to think this place was magical because of the way it made me feel when I was here. It wasn't until I got older that I realized it was the people that owned it that made it so special," Morgan told me fondly.

We hadn't even made it out of the truck before we had family and friends descending upon us. I recognized many of them since I knew all of Landon's side of the family already, but Morgan took the time to introduce me to his other aunts, uncles, and more cousins than I could keep track of. They were a loud family, each person trying to talk over the next, but I could tell how much they all loved each other and I immediately felt like I belonged.

Morgan led me around the back of the house and up the steps to an enormous wooden deck. From there I was able to see out further, to the trees and a creek that ran along the back of the property.

"Would you like something to drink?" he asked.

"Just a water, please," I answered. Morgan dug around in a cooler on the deck and handed me an icy cold bottle, keeping one for himself.

"There you two are!" I whipped around when I heard Landon's voice and smiled. Micah was with him and he had his arm draped over Landon's shoulders as they walked out of the house and towards us. "I was starting to get worried when I hadn't heard from either of you."

"Meaning, he wanted me to send out a search party," Micah whispered loudly out of the side of his mouth. Landon scowled at his fiancé, elbowing him in the stomach, but Micah never even flinched. He was an ex-Navy SEAL and he was about as tough as they came.

"What? It's true," Micah said with a laugh.

"Yes, but you don't have to tell them *everything*," Landon said, rolling his eyes.

"I haven't told them everything. I never said a word about what you and I got up to last night…" Landon quickly covered Micah's mouth with his hand and we all laughed as Micah grabbed his wrist and removed the hand easily. "I won't say a word, no matter how epic it was," he promised.

"It really was epic, wasn't it?" he whispered and the way he looked at his fiancé reminded me of one of those cartoon characters with the hearts spinning around their head. I cleared my throat and Landon turned his attention back to us.

"Anyway, then I talked to Aunt Susie who said that you two rode here together. When did you decide to do that?" Landon asked. I glanced over at Morgan who shrugged his shoulders as he took a sip of water.

"It was for the environment," I told Landon lamely before I could think through my response. Landon and Micah both looked completely confused while Morgan choked on the water he'd been drinking. It served him right for leaving me to answer on my own. He was still gasping for air when the door opened and Kathy and Rick Greene walked out, followed by a man and a woman I knew immediately had to be Morgan's parents.

Susie's face lit up when she saw Morgan and she ran to him. I smiled as he hugged her tightly. She was laughing and wiping tears at the same time as she stepped back to give Jeff a chance to hug his son. Morgan was smiling as he clapped his dad on the back and then he turned so that he could introduce me to his parents. I held out my hand, but they each ignored it as they took turns hugging me. I laughed as I was then passed on to Rick and Kathy Greene, but I was already used to their hugs. The Greenes were a very affectionate family and apparently, that extended beyond just their immediate family.

We made small talk and I found myself feeling very relaxed around Morgan's parents. They were kind, funny, and I liked them immediately. Morgan was the spitting image of his father, while Susie was shorter, with long, wavy blond hair, blue eyes, and a friendly smile. Landon's siblings and their significant others joined us and before long, talk turned to the wedding. I glanced around, only half listening and when my eyes landed on Morgan, I was surprised to see him staring at me. He winked at me and mouthed the words, *"Told you so."* I rolled my eyes, but couldn't stop the grin that spread across my face. Pleased that his parents seemed to like me just as he'd predicted.

After a while, everyone got busy preparing dinner. Rick and Jeff manned the grill while the rest of us helped carry the food out to the tables that were lined up on the deck. Once it was ready, everyone began filling their plates and gathered in small groups to eat. I was surprised to find that the meat was cooked perfectly instead of being burned beyond recognition. I chuckled as I wondered if Morgan's dad would be willing to teach my dad how to grill. Morgan gave me a questioning look, but I just waved him off.

It was dark out by the time we finished eating, visiting, and cleaning everything up for the next day. The rest of the family headed off to their various homes, hotels, and bedrooms inside the cabin for the night while Landon's siblings, their spouses, Morgan and I walked to where the guys had put together a bonfire near the woods at the back of the property. Chairs sat here and there around the area and Landon's brothers-in-law set down the cooler of beer they'd been carrying.

Carter's husband, Ryan, started the fire while Caleb turned on a radio then everyone grabbed a drink and settled in. It wasn't long before our laughter rang out through the night air as I listened to them share story after story from their childhoods.

"So, how's married life, Ryan? You sick of my brother yet?" Caleb asked. He was sitting across from me, snuggled up on Giovanni's lap. He grinned mischievously at his twin, Carter stuck his tongue out at him in return.

"Not yet, but give it a couple more months and ask me again," Ryan joked. Everyone laughed as Carter pretended to be wounded by his husband's words.

"You keep on talking like that, it's fine, but just look out because in a couple of months, we'll be on tour and I might just get the idea to call you out on stage in the middle of a show and serenade you in front of thousands of people," Carter threatened through narrowed eyes. He knew that his sexy husband did not share his love for the limelight.

"I'd like to change my answer," Ryan told Caleb quickly. "Being married to your brother is the stuff dreams are made of. I wake up to the sounds of birds singing and the sun shining every day," he added, laying it on extra thick.

"That's right, assholes. Being married to me is a gift from God and don't you forget it," Carter declared, looking around the fire at each of us.

It was quiet for just a beat and then we all roared with laughter. Well, all except Carter who folded his arms over his chest and pretended to pout. Ryan had his arm around the back of Carter's chair and he used it to pull Carter closer to him. He whispered something in Carter's ear and Carter's pout turned into a satisfied smile. He tilted his head and kissed his husband.

I smiled as I watched the happy couple. We all knew that the men were crazy about each other and that there were no other people in the world more perfectly suited for each other than the two of them. They had been lucky enough to find the one person they were meant to be with. My eyes swept over the couples surrounding the fire. It was a rare and wondrous thing when a person was able to find their soulmate, but each of the couples there that night had done exactly that. Well, everyone with the exception of me and Morgan.

I turned to where he was sitting beside me and once again, found his eyes fixed on me. One half of his face was in shadow, but the other was lit up by the glow of the fire. The look in his eyes was serious as if he had been trying to work through a difficult puzzle, but then it softened as he saw me looking back at him and he smiled. Morgan's smile had a way of warming me more than the fire had and I felt it all the way to my toes.

My thoughts turned to the night we had spent together, the way it felt as he slid inside me, our sweat-slickened bodies moving in a perfectly synchronized rhythm. Morgan's jaw clenched and the look in his eyes turned to liquid fire and I knew that he was having the same thoughts as me. My heartbeat quickened as that wonderful electrical charge that I'd come to associate with only Morgan, sprung to life and arced between us, connecting us in a way that wasn't meant for anyone else.

"Oh, God! Would you two knock it off already?" I jumped at the sound of Caleb's voice and we quickly turned to look across the fire.

I was worried that everyone around us had somehow been able to see the thoughts between Morgan and myself, but instead I saw Caleb groaning and covering his face as Carter and Ryan continued to make out. Everyone laughed because they knew that the twins were able to feel the strong emotions of each other and that Caleb was getting some pretty strong vibes from his brother, likely caused from the passion between Carter and Ryan.

We hung out for another hour, just talking and laughing until Micah stood and announced that he was going to take Landon to bed one last time before he was a married man. The party broke up after that and everyone began walking back towards the house. We all exchanged hugs and then Morgan and I climbed into his truck.

It had been a fun evening, full of good food, laughter, and amazing friends, which was exactly what Landon and Micah had asked for in place of a more traditional bachelor party. Before we'd even made it to the end of the driveway, Morgan was reaching for my hand and twining our fingers together.

CHAPTER
Ten

Akio

"ARE YOU TIRED?" MORGAN ASKED AS HE DROVE.

"No. I'm not tired at all after the nap I took earlier."

"Do you mind if we take a little drive then?" He glanced over at me with a hopeful smile, his face lit up by the lights of the dashboard. He was so handsome that it literally took my breath away sometimes.

"I don't mind at all," I told him and really, what other answer was there? I could be dying and I'd still go with him anywhere.

He turned at the next stop sign and the truck began making its way up a steep and winding road. The radio played some country song softly in the background and Morgan's thumb rubbed back and forth over my hand as he held it.

I hadn't seen any other cars since we'd turned onto that road and

I was beginning to wonder where he was taking me when he suddenly stopped and began backing into a narrow cut in the trees. I wasn't sure what he was doing since the area he was backing into wasn't even a road. He parked the truck and then looked at me with a broad smile.

"Come on, I want to show you something," he said excitedly.

Morgan opened his door and climbed out and I waited as he ran around to my side and opened the door for me. It was funny how in the short amount of time I'd known him, I'd already begun to expect those chivalrous gestures from him. It was nice and I wondered why no other guy I'd gone out with had ever taken the time to do those things for me. I knew some guys might get upset if their date opened doors for them, thinking the man they were with saw them as weak or too soft, but I knew that it was Morgan's way of showing me respect and care and I felt valued and cherished when he did it.

I jumped down from the truck and smiled up at him. I didn't know what he was up to, but his excitement was contagious. He took my hand and led me to the back of the truck and I gasped as I saw the sight before me. The trees had opened up and I was standing in a clearing, on the side of a mountain.

He let go of my hand and I could hear him doing something with his truck, but I couldn't be bothered to see what because I was too busy taking in the spectacular view. The sky was full of stars and the moon shone bright, allowing me to see for miles. The surrounding mountains jutted up to the sky at varying intervals and below us was a town, all lit up and looking like it belonged on a postcard.

"This is amazing!" I said over my shoulder. "How did you even find this place?"

"A friend of mine told me about it when we were in high school. He used to bring his dates up here to fool around," he explained with a chuckle.

"I can see where this would be a good make out spot. So, did you bring a lot of dates up here too?" I teased and then regretted it immediately as my stomach sank at the thought of him with anyone else. I wasn't stupid, I knew that neither one of us were virgins, but that didn't mean I wanted to think about him in another man's arms. The thought alone had me wanting to scratch somebody's eyes out.

Morgan moved up behind me and pulled me against him. The heat from his chest soaked through my back, warming my entire body. The rough feel of his calloused hands rubbing up and down my arms sent chills up my spine and I shivered.

"Are you cold?" he whispered in my ear.

"No," I answered simply.

"In answer to your question, no. I've never brought anyone up here before." I felt my body relax and I leaned back into him, loving the way he wrapped his arms around me and kissed the side of my head. "I have spent a lot of time up here by myself though. I used to come up here so I could be alone to think. Especially right before I left…"

His voice trailed off and I could feel his body tense against mine. I still didn't know what had made him decide to leave, but I could tell by the way he had reacted the few times it had come up that it had been difficult and not something he was ready to talk about just yet.

"So, if this is your private thinking spot, what made you decide to bring me here? Not that I don't appreciate the gesture or the view," I hurried to assure him.

"I don't know," he admitted quietly. "I guess I just wanted to share it with you; to let you see a part of me that no one else knows." I turned in his arms so that I could see his face. His eyes were soft as he looked down at me and I thought I could see the same feelings I had for him, reflected back at me. *Could he really be falling for me too?* My heart beat against my rib cage at the thought.

"Thank you," I whispered. I hoped that he could tell in those two little words how much it meant that he had shared something so special with me, but I pulled him down for a kiss in order to make my message clearer.

My eyes slid shut as Morgan's lips covered mine in a kiss that obliterated the memory of any kiss that had ever come before. My hands fisted in his hair as he bit down gently on my bottom lip and tugged then began kissing his way down my neck. I threw my head back with a moan as he bit down on the sensitive skin between my neck and shoulder and a bolt of lust shot directly from that area to my cock.

My hands travelled down over his broad back, feeling the deliciously hard muscles as they moved under the fabric of his t-shirt, but it wasn't enough. I needed to be able to feel his bare skin beneath my fingertips so I began tugging at the material. Understanding my intent, Morgan grasped the hem of his shirt in both hands and yanked it up and over his head, letting it fall to the ground without a thought. His breaths were ragged as he watched me run my hands over the hard plains of his chest and down over his rock-hard abs. I got to his belt and paused with my hands over the buckle.

"I want to taste you," I told him, pleased when I heard his quick intake of air.

"I'm all yours," he said in a shaky voice. I averted my eyes quickly. I knew he hadn't meant it in *that* way and I didn't want him to see how much I wished he had. But oh, the thought of Morgan Greene being all mine…

I made quick work of his belt and then dropped to my knees right there on the ground. I undid his jeans and then worked them over his hips and down to his knees. His briefs soon followed and my mouth watered at the sight of his long, thick cock leaking in front of me. Circling my hand around the base, I lapped at his offering, moaning when I tasted the salty liquid. My lips wrapped around the bulbous head and I sucked him into my mouth slowly, increasing the suction as I went. I kept going until I had sucked him all the way down, his cock filling my throat and cutting off my air. I held there until my eyes watered and my lungs cried out for air and then I pulled off with a loud, wet sound.

I peered up at him as I swirled my tongue around the tip and held his gaze as I pulled him back in my mouth, swallowing his cock hungrily. Sweat was dripping down the center of his chest, his jaw was clenched tightly and I could see the struggle etched on his face as he fought to hold back. I didn't want him to hold back though; I wanted him to give me everything he had. I let him slide out of my mouth, but continued to work my hand up and down his length as I stared at him.

"You said you were all mine for the night, so quit holding back." My voice sounded hoarse from having my throat stretched.

"I won't hurt you," he growled.

"I want you to fuck my mouth. I want it all," I demanded. I waited until he gave me a single nod and then I slid him back inside my mouth, savoring the fresh burst of pre-cum my words had brought about.

Morgan moved his hips slowly at first, but soon he gave in to his urges and gripped the back of my head as he began sliding his cock back and forth quickly into my eager mouth. He looked exquisite with his head thrown back and his mouth hanging open as his hips thrust forward in wild abandon. His pleasure became my own as I let him use my body to seek his fulfillment.

"I have to stop," he groaned, halting his movements and pulling me off him. He gripped the base of his cock tightly and I grinned up at him proudly as I gasped for air. I liked knowing that it was me that made him lose control like that and no one else.

"Come here," he said after he'd gained control. He reached under my arms and lifted me. His mouth slammed down on mine as soon as I was on my feet, his tongue sweeping into my mouth and I wondered if he could taste himself on my tongue.

I wrapped my arms around his neck while his hands began to explore my body. Morgan paused long enough to pull my shirt over my head and then continued to devour my mouth. My body thrummed with anticipation when his hand dipped below the waistband of my jeans and he ran one finger up and down my crack, circling my pucker and awakening the nerves there. My eyes rolled up in my head as he stuck just the tip of one finger inside me.

"More," I pleaded, but instead he pulled his hand out of my pants. I growled with frustration and his eyes met mine. They were full of passion and excitement.

"Don't worry, baby. I'm nowhere near done with you yet," he informed me and his lips lifted in a feral grin.

A tremor shook my body as he instructed me to take off my pants and I hurried to do his bidding as he kicked off his shoes and finished undressing himself. When we were finally undressed, we paused for just a moment to admire each other's naked forms in the moonlight and then we came together in a passionate kiss that threatened to consume both of us.

Morgan lifted me and I wrapped my legs around his waist as he carried me over to his truck and lowered me onto the tailgate. I braced myself for the feel of the cold metal against my skin, but instead, I landed on something soft and I realized what he'd been doing while I'd been admiring the scenic view. I pulled my mouth from his and looked in the truck bed behind me then back at him, quirking my eyebrow.

"I thought you didn't bring dates up here to fool around," I joked. Morgan shrugged his shoulders.

"Maybe I was just waiting for the right person to share this place with," he said quietly.

My heart leapt in my chest, but I didn't have time to think about his words before he wrapped his hand around both of our cocks and began sliding it up and down. The dual sensations of his rough palm stroking us and the silky feel of his cock against mine was enough to make me lose my mind.

"Lie back," he instructed. I lowered myself onto my back and watched as he picked up a packet of lube that I hadn't even noticed was lying on the blanket beside me and I gave him a questioning look. "I was hoping," he answered, wearing that smirk that always made my brain feel fuzzy.

He tore open the packet and coated his fingers before rubbing them over my entrance. I spread my legs wider as he pressed his fingers inside me, gently working me open. I groaned when he found my prostate and rubbed over it, sending a shockwave of electricity racing through my veins. Then I felt the wet heat of his mouth as it closed over the head of my dick and I tossed my head from side to side.

"Morgan, please," I begged. I wasn't even sure what I was begging for at that point, I just knew I wanted him to be on top of me, around me, and inside me all at once. I wanted him to consume me.

"Okay, baby. I've got you," he assured me.

He worked quickly, rolling the condom on and then lubing his shaft. I was shaking with need as he entered me. Morgan eased in slowly so he wouldn't hurt me, whispering words of encouragement as my body accepted his thick cock. Once he was all the way in, he grabbed my ankles and raised them up to rest on his shoulders.

"You ready, baby?" he asked.

"Yes! I need you, Morgan," I said and then cried out as he began rocking his hips.

He pulled nearly all the way out and then slammed back in, stealing the breath from my lungs and sending me closer and closer to the edge. I heard his change in breathing and his movements quickened and I knew he was close as well, so I reached down and grasped my cock in my hand and began stroking it in time with his thrusts.

Sweat dripped off his forehead, landing on my stomach and he adjusted his angle so that he was hitting my prostate with each thrust. That was enough to put me over the edge and I came, screaming his name up into the night sky. He followed seconds later with a loud moan and then he bent his body over mine, resting his forehead on my stomach as he caught his breath.

My pulse was still racing as I reached for him, combing my

fingers through his sweat-soaked hair. He pulled out gently and tied the condom, laying it to the side then he began licking his way up my body, cleaning the cum off my chest with his tongue. When he was done, he climbed into the truck with me and lay down beside me, grabbing another blanket and covering us up with it.

I snuggled into his side and he kissed the top of my head as we gazed at the stars overhead. Neither one of us felt the need to speak, our bodies sated and blissfully numb, and I thought to myself that I couldn't remember ever feeling happier or more peaceful than I did in that moment. I was no longer falling for Morgan, but was in fact, one hundred percent, completely in love with him. My last thought as I drifted off was that I hoped he'd be there to catch me.

I checked to make sure my tie was lying straight and smoothed my hands over the light gray material of my suit. Satisfied that I was presentable, I stepped away from the full-length mirror and opened the bedroom door. I heard another door opening at the end of the hall and turned my head in time to see Morgan stepping out of the bathroom, the tantalizing scent of his aftershave lingering in the air.

I made a show of eyeing him up and down, before holding a finger in the air and making the motion for him to turn around. He smirked at me, but held his arms out to the sides as he slowly spun around for my perusal. He was wearing a black suit that showed off his broad shoulders and narrow waist perfectly. His tie was a sea-green color that matched his eyes and I was pleased to see that he had left the scruff on his face per my request.

"Mmm, mmm, mmm," I hummed out slowly, showing my approval. I bit my lip as he swiveled back around to face me and he looked down at the floor, but not before I saw his pleased smile. He was usually the more brazen of the two of us and I found myself charmed by his newfound shyness.

"You look so handsome," I told him, sincerely.

"Thank you, but no one will be able to even look at anyone else once you step foot in the room." Morgan came towards me and lifted my chin with a finger so that he could kiss me. I gripped his elbows as I swayed on my feet and I wondered how terribly upset Landon would be if we were late for his wedding.

"We need to go. Now!" Morgan said gruffly and I laughed, knowing that he'd been thinking the same thing as me.

We were halfway to the cabin when Morgan's phone rang and he put it on speaker. Susie sounded panicked as she explained to us that the florist had already set up the flowers for the wedding, but had forgotten to leave Landon and Micah's boutonnieres when she left. They'd tried calling her, but her phone must have been dead because she wasn't picking up and could we please swing by her shop in town and get the flowers?

Morgan assured his mom that he would get the flowers and be there in time for the wedding and then he hung up, turning around quickly so he could head into town. It didn't take long for us to get there and my eyes widened when I saw it.

"I told you it was small," Morgan chuckled.

"Yeah, but I expected there to be at least more than one stoplight," I said, laughing.

"Hey! We're pretty big now. I'll have you know that we got our first McDonald's a few years ago. The next town over doesn't even have that. They have to drive all the way here if they want to get a burger," he said proudly and I died laughing. Morgan shook his head at me, but he couldn't keep from laughing with me.

We were still laughing when we pulled up outside of the flower shop and got out. I looked at the sign painted on the large picture window which read: *Kim's Flower Garden, where everything comes up rosy*. This of course, left me in a fit of giggles because of the sheer corniness, but Morgan just opened the door, whispering at me to please behave. I straightened my face, but a part of me wanted to push it just to see if I could get him to spank me again.

Morgan explained what had happened to the owner, who kept apologizing profusely and insisted on giving us coupons for free flowers. Morgan thanked her, but told her all we really needed were the flowers for the grooms. She gathered them quickly, apologizing the entire time and handed them to us, along with the aforementioned coupons. We thanked her again and then turned to leave.

"Well, now I can see why they say everything's so rosy in here," I whispered so only Morgan could hear and he grabbed my hand and pulled me from the shop, shutting the door behind us so poor Miss Kim wouldn't hear our laughter.

We were on our way to the truck when I heard Morgan's laughter cut off. I looked up at him to see what was going on and was surprised to see his face etched in an unfamiliar mask. His eyes were dark and his jaw was clenched as if he were angry. I looked around to try and figure out what had put that look on his face and my eyes landed on two men who were stopped in the middle of the sidewalk only a few feet away from us. They were both staring at Morgan and the looks on their faces were a mixture between shock, sadness, curiosity, and something else that I couldn't quite put my finger on.

I watched the taller man, a blond who looked like he could be a body builder as his eyes shifted back and forth between Morgan and me, landing on where our hands were clasped. He smiled at the two of us, but I noticed it didn't quite reach his eyes.

The other man was a bit rougher looking, with dark hair and lines around his eyes and mouth. He looked me up and down slowly and I felt Morgan tense beside me. I wasn't sure what the situation was between the three of them, but I stepped closer to Morgan in a show of solidarity.

"Morgan, I didn't realize you were back in town. Are you visiting Susie and Jeff?" the blond asked.

"I'm here for Landon's wedding," Morgan answered quietly.

"Ah, I see. I'm David by the way," he said, sticking his hand out towards me. I glanced up at Morgan, but his face betrayed nothing.

"Akio," I told him, having no choice but to shake his hand.

"It's nice to meet you, Akio. I'm Bryan," the dark-haired man said. He stuck his hand out as well, but I heard Morgan growl low in his throat.

"We need to go," he informed them, his voice hard and cold and I watched, stunned, as he turned and walked to the truck and climbed inside.

I followed him, shutting my door behind me. I'd barely gotten my seatbelt on when Morgan pulled away from the curb and sped through town. I looked in the side mirror and noticed the two men were turned and watching us as we drove away.

"What was that all about?" I asked.

"Nothing," he answered curtly.

"Who were those two guys?" I pressed. I had never seen him so upset and I wanted to try and help if I could, but I needed to know what was going on first. Morgan huffed out a breath, sounding frustrated, but I wasn't sure if it was with me or the situation.

"David is my ex," he told me and I felt my stomach roll.

"And Bryan?" I asked quietly.

"I don't know him. Not sure I ever did," he answered in a clipped tone.

Morgan was quiet the rest of the drive and I left him alone, hoping that having time to sort his thoughts would help, but warning signs were going off in my head telling me that something wasn't right.

CHAPTER
Eleven

Morgan

THE DRIVE TO THE CABIN WAS A BLUR TO ME, MY BRAIN switching over to autopilot so that I could continue to function even though my body felt like it was in shock. I suppose venturing into the main part of town, I should have expected to run into them, but I'd been so caught up in Akio that suddenly coming face to face with David and Bryan had felt like a slap in the face.

I hated the fact that Akio had been there to witness the exchange between David, Bryan, and myself and I knew he had to have a lot more questions running around in his head, but I couldn't bring myself to answer those questions just yet. I wasn't sure of the details, but I could tell that Akio had been hurt in the past and I wanted to make sure he and I were stronger before he learned about my failed relationship with David so I wouldn't scare him off.

I pulled in the driveway and quickly parked. The wedding would be starting soon and I knew my mom was probably freaking out that we weren't there yet. I jumped out of the truck and tried to stop my hands from shaking as I grabbed the flowers off the back seat. I was halfway up the front steps when I heard Akio's door shut. I glanced over my shoulder at him and there was a hurt look on his face that nearly brought me to my knees, but the door swung open just then and my mom and Aunt Kathy were there, looking relieved. They grabbed the flowers out of my hands and told us to hurry out back and find a seat because the wedding was about to start.

I turned to Akio, but he was gone. I raced down the porch steps and saw his retreating form as he rounded the corner of the house and stepped into the backyard. I followed and slid into the empty chair next to him. Everyone else was already seated and waiting for the grooms, their soft murmuring and the gentle sound of music could be heard throughout the yard which had been decorated with flowers at the end of each row of chairs and a beautiful archway that was draped in delicate white tulle with tiny fire and ice roses interwoven in it.

I glanced at Akio out of the corner of my eye, but he was looking straight ahead, his face unreadable. Caleb and Carter drew my attention as they began walking slowly down the center aisle, escorting their mother to her seat and looking like two perfectly matched bookends. They each kissed her cheek and then made their way to the back again where they retraced their steps, but this time Caleb walked next to his husband, Giovanni, who would be standing up with Micah as his best man and Carter walked beside Lachlan who was Micah's other best man.

When they reached the end, they took their places on either side of the archway then the music swelled and everyone stood as Landon and Micah made their way down the aisle, hand in hand. We sat back down as they stood under the archway and turned to face each other.

They made a very handsome couple with Landon in a black suit and Micah in his Navy SEALs white dress uniform.

Landon blinked rapidly and I could tell that he was trying to fight back tears, but Micah reached forward and brushed away the one that managed to escape with his thumb and whispered something to him, making Landon laugh. They exchanged vows that they had written themselves and I could hear sniffling as Micah promised to protect not only Landon's body, but his heart, mind, and soul. Landon then told Micah that he was the most important person in his life and that he promised to always treat Micah and their marriage with all the love and respect that they deserved.

I felt Akio stiffen next to me and I turned to look at him, wondering what about Landon's words had upset him, but the mask he'd been wearing before was firmly back in place, giving me no clue as to what he was thinking. I hated the tension that was currently between us, but I wasn't sure what I could do to fix it without having to explain everything that had happened between David and myself.

I looked back towards the front as I heard the minister announce Landon and Micah as Mr. and Mr. Greene, Micah having chosen to take Landon's name rather than keep a last name he said meant nothing to him anymore. I stood along with everyone else and clapped my hands, pasting on a smile that I hoped didn't look as fake as it felt.

The wedding party along with Landon's parents and sisters began taking pictures with the photographer while the rest of us moved to the tables that had been set up under a tent for the reception. I sat down next to Akio, but he quickly turned and began talking with the other members of Carter's band. I listened with half an ear as they discussed the upcoming tour, but my mind kept wandering back to my run-in with David and Bryan, which led to thoughts of the past. I stopped a server as he walked by and grabbed a drink from his tray, hoping it would help take the edge off so I could relax and enjoy the rest of the evening.

Once the photographer was finished, the grooms joined the party and we all cheered them as they entered the tent. Dinner was served and while I'm sure it was delicious to everyone else, it tasted like chalk to me so I settled for a second drink. By my third or maybe my fourth glass of wine, I was feeling much more relaxed and I found myself laughing at everything the people at my table said. I caught a few concerned looks being thrown my way from Akio, but I ignored them because I was finally feeling good again and I didn't want anything to upset that delicate balance.

Landon and Micah shared their first dance as a married couple and I laughed hysterically when they shoved cake in each other's faces. No one else seemed to think it was as funny as I did. I watched as Akio stood and walked over to Landon and Micah. He spoke to them for a minute and I stiffened when all three of them glanced my way, but then they smiled and hugged him and he turned and began walking back towards me.

I asked Akio if he wanted to dance, even though I'd never been a very good dancer, but he told me that he was tired and just wanted to leave. I stood and dug my keys out of my pocket, but he moved quickly, snatching them out of my hand. I started to protest, but he grabbed my hand and pulled me outside of the tent. As we walked around the house to my truck, I felt the first genuine smile I'd had on my face that night because I was holding Akio's hand and it felt good and it felt perfect and it felt right.

I woke the next morning in my bed at my parents' house. The sunlight streaming through the windows hurt my eyes and I groaned at the pounding in my head. Flashes of the day before began filtering through and I groaned again. I'd had too much to drink at the wedding, but it had helped me to forget about the past. Of course, in the light of day those memories all came rushing back, refusing to be silenced.

I parked my truck outside our house, but instead of getting out, I let my head drop back and closed my eyes. It had been an exhausting day at work, but somehow, I'd managed to leave early which almost never happened, especially considering we'd been shorthanded. Three of my crew members had been out sick, including my foreman and best friend. He'd been sick a lot lately and I was starting to get concerned. I knew he hated going to the doctor, but I might just have to make him.

My thoughts drifted to David and I opened my eyes, seeing his car in the driveway. As tired as I was, I knew I needed to spend some time with him. We'd grown up in the same small town and had been friends for years, but it wasn't until a party we'd both been at two years before that we had decided to go out on a date. It had made sense at the time. We enjoyed the same activities, we already knew we got along, and I thought he was cute.

We went mountain biking on our first date and when we kissed at the end of the night it was good; not earth-shattering, but good, comforting. We continued dating and had a lot of fun together, it was like having your best friend around, but getting to enjoy sexy times too. I assumed I loved him, I wasn't sure because I'd never been in love before, but I had fun with him and liked spending time with him and I cared about him a lot. Wasn't that what love was?

After a while though, I began noticing that David didn't seem as happy anymore. He assured me that he was just busy at work and that once the project he was working on was finished then he'd be able to relax. Once his project ended though, things seemed to get worse. I would catch him staring off into space when we were watching movies together and there seemed to be long stretches of silence where neither of us seemed to be able to think of anything to say. It was uncomfortable and made me feel like I was crawling out of my skin, so I began taking on more jobs so I could avoid the awkwardness I felt whenever we were together. I hated it though and I missed my friend and the easy way we used to banter back and forth and the fun we used to have.

Looking for anything that might help, I asked David if he wanted to move in with me. The smile he'd given me was glorious and I knew I'd done the right thing. I'd convinced myself that moving in together would help us get back on track. Things were much better for the first three months, we each made an effort to get home early from work so we could have dinner together and then we'd usually curl up on the couch together and watch TV. Our sex life picked back up, we spent our weekends doing the things we'd always loved doing together like hiking, fishing, and mountain climbing and it felt like we were finally back to normal; things were good.

Then I signed a contract to build a huge chain store and David started a new project at his design firm and the next thing I knew we were back to spending no time together. We began to fight over the tiniest things, like him leaving his socks on the floor or me forgetting to take out the trash and it felt like things were even worse than they'd been before. I hated it and I missed my friend, but I wasn't sure what to do to fix it. I asked David, but he seemed even more distant when he told me he wasn't sure things could be fixed. I didn't believe that though and so I'd left work early that day with the intention of taking him to our favorite restaurant and then coming home and making love. Maybe spending a little time together was all we needed to reconnect.

I let out a tired sigh and climbed out of my truck. I walked up the sidewalk to the front porch, making a mental note that I needed to mow the grass. We'd been neglecting the yard since we'd both been working so much, but maybe that weekend David and I could spend some time fixing it up and making it look nice again. The thought of everything that needed fixing right then was almost overwhelming so I decided to focus on one thing at a time. My priority at that moment: David.

I walked in the front door and called out his name, but there was no answer so I headed down the hall to our bedroom. I heard water running as I passed the bathroom and then a long, loud moan and I smiled; it sounded like David was enjoying himself in the shower.

I quickly stripped my shirt off and opened the door, planning on joining him, but my blood turned to ice in my veins when I saw two figures behind the shower curtain. I still had the biggest surprise in store though when I yanked the curtain aside and found David with Bryan, my foreman and best friend.

I felt hurt and angry and betrayed and all I could think about was getting away from them so I stormed out, ignoring their calls and went to my parents' house. Luckily, Mom and Dad seemed to sense that I needed space so they hugged me and then left me to wallow in my misery. I went back to work after a few days and felt nauseous when I immediately came face to face with Bryan. Even the regret I saw in his eyes didn't make me feel any better, it was just a glaring reminder of what he'd done to me and to our friendship. I told him that he was fired and I watched in stony silence as he nodded his head sadly and went to his office to gather his things.

When I went home that night, David was sitting on the couch waiting for me. He shot to his feet and started to approach me, but I stuck out a hand to stop him. I couldn't handle the thought of him touching me. We sat down and I listened silently as he told me that he'd been feeling adrift for a long time, that he knew that something wasn't right between us and then he'd started talking to Bryan.

He explained that at first, they talked about me. David had been trying to understand what he could do to bridge the gap that had formed between us and he thought since Bryan was my best friend and we worked together that he might be able to help. He was more than happy to help, I'd thought snidely.

David told me that the more they talked, the more they began to care about each other and eventually, one thing led to another. I cut him off at that point because I couldn't stand to hear it and told him that apparently, there was nothing else to say and that I wanted him to leave. He looked sad as he stood up and walked out the door. The sound of it shutting behind him echoed throughout the room and I curled up onto the couch and fell asleep, my tears leaving salty tracks down my cheeks.

Running into them in our tiny town was inevitable, but every time it happened it felt like the wound had been ripped back open. Sure, David and I had been having problems, but I hadn't thought that they were so bad that they couldn't be fixed. The fact that we had been friends for years had made the possibility of him cheating on me seem impossible. Add in the fact that not only had David cheated, but it had been with another person who I had trusted completely and I was devastated.

Eventually, I started to realize that having David gone from my home didn't feel that different than when he'd been living there. It slowly began to sink in that I wasn't as upset about breaking up with David as I was hurt that my two "friends" had betrayed me and broken my trust. I was finally able to understand what David had been telling me; that our relationship had been over for a long time. That knowledge made me sad, but it also allowed me to start to heal and move on.

However, being lied to by people I'd trusted was a harder pill to swallow and not something I would ever be able to understand. Then came the day when the news of their engagement reached me and I lost it. Anger filled me and I got drunk and ended up punching a hole in a wall at the bar I was in. The bartender called my dad who came and picked me up and drove me home.

Dad stayed there all night, watching over me as I slept off the alcohol on the couch. The next morning, we had a long talk where I finally told him everything that had happened. He wrapped an arm around me and held me as I cried, getting all the hurt out of my system and then I listened as he quietly yet firmly reminded me of who I was and where I came from and that the bitterness and resentment that had been consuming me was not what my life was supposed to be about. He told me that I had too much goodness inside me to waste it on people who couldn't even comprehend what loyalty and friendship were all about.

I made a decision that day, not an easy one and not one that my parents were thrilled about, but one that they understood was necessary for my healing. I decided to move from the only place I'd ever called home and go to Chicago where I'd be able to start over and not have David and Bryan's relationship thrown in my face on a daily basis. It was hard on my parents to see their only child leaving, but it helped them to know that I would have the love and support of my cousins and aunt and uncle who lived close, not too far from my new home.

Moving to Chicago ended up being the best decision I could have made because my business was growing more quickly than I had hoped but it also led me to meeting Akio. I felt myself smile as I thought about the man sleeping across the hall.

Akio was gorgeous and I had been attracted to him from the very start, but what I had thought would be a harmless bit of fun and flirting, soon turned into something more. Being with him was always full of surprises because I never knew what he was going to say or do, but in the best possible ways. Akio was an intelligent man with a sharp wit and an even sharper tongue. He was thoughtful and compassionate and his relationships with his friends and family proved what an honest and loving man he was.

Then there was the way he made me feel. I'd never experienced anything like the chemistry between the two of us, but instead of cooling down after our first time together, it seemed to get even more intense the closer we became. It was more than just my physical reaction to him though. When I was with Akio I felt happy and important and like I could take on the entire world.

When I'd walked in and caught David and Bryan together, I'd felt pissed off and betrayed, but those feelings were nothing compared to the protectiveness I'd felt when Akio and David shook hands or the rage I'd felt as I watched Bryan extend his hand. Akio was everything pure and light and happy and they had no right to touch him and cast their shadows onto him. I'd barely tolerated him and David shaking hands, but there was no way I was going to let Bryan touch what was mine ever again. *Mine.* I let that thought settle into my mind.

Akio was mine.

My relationship with Akio was the complete opposite of my relationship with David, and maybe that was why things seemed to be working out so much better. At least I hoped they were, I know I owed him an apology for my behavior the night before, as well as answers about my past. I didn't like thinking about that time, but Akio deserved to know, especially if I wanted him to be a part of my future. I realized in that moment exactly how much I really did want him in my future because I was completely head over heels in love with the man.

I rolled over in my bed, eager to wake Akio and tell him everything, but I stopped when I saw the piece of paper that was lying on the table by my bed. My pulse quickened as I reached for it and then turned to sludge as I read his words.

Morgan,
There was an emergency at work and I needed to take the first flight back to Chicago. I didn't want to wake you so I let you sleep. Please thank your parents for me and be careful driving back.

–Akio

I knew I had been distant the day before, but I wasn't sure what I had done that would cause him to leave. All I knew was that I wasn't buying his excuse about a work emergency. Of course, I couldn't verify any of it with Landon because he was on his honeymoon, but I had a gut instinct that something bigger was going on. Without another thought, I grabbed my bag and began packing. It was time to go home.

CHAPTER
Twelve

Akio

M Y PHONE BUZZED IN MY POCKET AND I PULLED IT OUT, my heart squeezing in my chest when I saw who it was. Morgan had called and texted many times over the past week and I'd managed to ignore it, but it was getting harder and harder as time went on.

On the ride from town to the wedding, I'd fought the urge to ask the hundreds of questions that were running through my head, particularly regarding Morgan's ex, David.

David.

Even thinking his name made me want to throw up. I'd never been the jealous type or at least I hadn't realized I was because I'd never had anyone to be jealous over, but just picturing Morgan and David together had me wanting to rip the man's hair out.

Then there was the way Morgan had reacted to seeing the two men. It was obvious that things between him and David hadn't ended well, but what did Bryan have to do with it and why had Morgan acted like he didn't want Bryan to shake hands with me? Was Morgan upset that David had moved on after they broke up? How long ago had they broken up and whose idea had it been? Was David the reason Morgan decided to leave Tennessee?

Then there were the questions that hurt most of all, but that I needed the answers to. Questions such as, where did I fit into all of it? Was I just a rebound guy? Someone to help Morgan pass the time until the right man came along or until David decided to take him back? Those were the questions that had kept me up every night since I'd returned home, but unfortunately, the only man that could answer them was the one person I was trying desperately to avoid.

It wasn't that I didn't want to see Morgan, in fact, I missed him, more than I'd ever thought possible, but I had to stay away from him to protect myself. I'd been burned too many times before by men who I thought cared about me, only to realize that I'd been nothing more than a place-holder for the men they really wanted to be with. The good-for-now guy, that's who I'd always been and it didn't look like things were going to be any different with Morgan. Just for once I'd like to be someone's good-for-ever guy.

I sighed as I shut off my phone and shoved it back in my pocket. I knew I was going to have to face Morgan eventually, we were working on the project together after all and there was no way I was going to slack off on my obligations to my friends or to Agape House. I just needed time to figure out how I was supposed to resist the man that had stolen my heart and made it his own.

I did my best to push all thoughts of Morgan aside as I pulled the door to the restaurant open and stepped inside. My eyes searched the room and finally landed on my friends. I'd have much rather spent the night curled up on my couch, binge watching *Orange is the New Black*, but Travis had called and insisted that I meet them for dinner and drinks after work.

I'd tried to tell him no, but he'd actually sounded hurt when he mentioned that I hadn't gone out with them in over four weeks. I'd been surprised by that and then I realized he was right and that I'd been so caught up with Morgan and work that I'd neglected my friends. I apologized and he told me just to make sure I was at the restaurant that night. So, there I was. I pasted on a smile and walked over to the table where the three of them sat. They looked up and smiled as I slid into the booth beside Garrett.

"Hey, man! How are you?" Jasper asked.

"Good. I'm good," I said, nodding my head for emphasis then groaned inwardly when I saw the knowing looks they shared with each other.

The thing about having people in your life that you'd been friends with for years, was that they knew everything about you and they could easily tell when something was wrong. Sometimes that was a blessing, but in my case, it was a curse. Especially because I knew they wouldn't let it drop just because I asked them to.

"We can tell something's wrong no matter how much you deny it," Travis said.

"Talk to us, we're your friends," Jasper reminded me.

"Yeah, maybe we can help," Garrett offered.

I felt a genuine smile spread across my face that time. Those guys may be a pain in the butt sometimes, but they had always been really good friends to me. I knew they cared about me and they were concerned so I took a deep breath and began telling them everything, from meeting Morgan and the work he was doing to the double date we'd been surprised to find ourselves on, all the way through the wedding and my decision to fly back home on my own.

The only parts I left out were the fact that I was in love with Morgan and the intimate moments he and I had shared together because no matter what happened between us, those moments were mine and no one else had a right to them. Those were the moments that I would carry in my heart forever. I finished telling them my story and took a sip of my margarita then sat back and waited for them to talk. I didn't have to wait long.

"You've been seeing this guy for weeks and this is the first we're hearing about it?" Jasper complained.

"Do I need to kick his ass?" Travis growled and it made me smile because that was typical Travis. He was the most laid-back of all of us, but mess with one of his friends and he turned into a fierce mother bear, protecting her cub.

"I'm sorry I didn't say something sooner; the whole thing just kind of took me by surprise. Also, I've been really busy between the Agape House project and helping Landon with the tour schedule before his wedding," I explained. Jasper nodded once then leaned back in his seat, looking appeased by my answer. I turned my attention to Travis who was still clenching his jaw.

"Calm down, there's no reason to kick his ass. We were just having some fun anyway," I said, shrugging my shoulders.

A lump formed in my throat and I nearly choked on the lie. It had been so much more than simple fun, for me at least. I grabbed my drink and took another long sip, licking the salt from my lips. I looked up and found all three sets of eyes on me.

"What?" I asked cautiously.

"This guy was different, wasn't he? You really liked him," Jasper said gently. I was mortified to feel my eyes beginning to burn and I reached down and pinched my leg so I'd have something else to focus on besides the clawing pain in my chest. It had hurt so badly to walk away from Morgan, but it was better than watching him walk away from me when he found someone else, I reminded myself.

"It doesn't matter because I'm not seeing him anymore," I said firmly, hoping they'd take the hint and drop it. It was quiet for a few minutes and then Travis winked at me and started talking about some guy he'd gone home with the night before. I gave him a small smile as a way of thanking him and then let myself relax into my seat.

I absentmindedly ran my finger over the rim of my glass as I glanced around the room, only half listening to Travis's story. It wasn't his fault though, Travis was usually quite entertaining. I just hadn't been able to concentrate on much of anything that past week. It was like my mind couldn't settle on any one thing because it was always being pulled in the opposite direction of where I wanted it to go. No matter how hard I tried to force them away, thoughts of Morgan always crept in.

My head turned and I caught Garrett staring at me. He averted his gaze quickly, but not before I saw the look in his eyes. He'd looked concerned and maybe a little disappointed. I'd noticed that he'd been unusually quiet as I'd told them about Morgan and I wondered what he was thinking. Was he disappointed in me for falling for the wrong guy once again?

I couldn't say that I blamed him if that were the case because I was disappointed too. There was a part of me that had truly believed that Morgan was different, that the way he'd looked at me and the way he'd held me had meant the same to him as it did to me. But his actions had made it clear that I wasn't as important to him as I'd thought.

There was another part of me that kept whispering that maybe I should have given him a break, that he was obviously upset and hadn't been acting like himself. That was the part that had me reaching for my phone about a million times over the last week, begging me to call him and give him a chance to explain. I'd lost count of the number of times I'd read through our texts or listened to the messages he'd left on my phone just so I could hear his voice, but then I'd remind myself that I was saving myself more pain by cutting things off right then.

Of course, we still had a job to do, but so far, I'd managed to stop by the job site when I knew Morgan wouldn't be there, discussing the progress of the rebuild with his foreman instead of him. I berated myself over my cowardly behavior, but I knew how weak I was around him and I couldn't risk getting sucked in again by his charm.

I didn't blame Morgan for what had happened. He was a wonderful man and it wasn't his fault that he didn't feel as strongly for me as I felt for him. I hated that things hadn't worked out between us, but that didn't mean he didn't deserve to find someone someday that was right for him. My heart squeezed painfully at the thought and I reached up and rubbed a hand over my chest, trying to ease the sharp ache.

My friends continued to laugh and talk throughout dinner and I jumped into the conversation here and there so they wouldn't notice how depressed I was. I waited until we'd paid the bill and then I stood and told them that I needed to go home and get some sleep.

"Come on, Grandpa, it's still early. Let's head over to Lush-Us," Travis pleaded.

"Nah, you guys go on without me. I've got work to do tomorrow since Landon's gone so I need to head out," I explained.

"I'll walk you out," Garrett said as he slid out of the booth.

I leaned down and hugged Travis and blew kisses to Jasper since I couldn't reach him then I walked out with Garrett following close behind. I took a deep breath of night air as I stepped outside the restaurant and fought back a yawn. A week of not sleeping was starting to catch up to me, making me feel like the old man Travis had accused me of being.

"Are you sure you're alright?" Garrett asked and I spun around to look at him.

"Yeah, I'll be fine. I'm just more tired than I realized. I just need a good night's sleep," I assured him.

"Let me drive you home," he suggested.

"No, I can walk. It's not far and it'll do me good to get some fresh air," I told him.

"Don't be ridiculous, Akio, you can barely stand up. I'm taking you home." I saw the determination in his eyes and I was too tired to argue so I nodded my head and followed him to his car. It only took a few minutes to reach my building and I yawned again as I took my seatbelt off. Garrett started to turn off the car, but I stopped him with my hand.

"I appreciate you driving me home, it probably wouldn't have been a good idea for me to walk home as tired as I am, but I think I can manage to make it inside my apartment on my own," I joked.

"I just thought you might want some company," he said quietly. He must have noticed the confused look on my face because he continued. "I know you were upset earlier and I didn't want you to be alone," he explained. I felt a warmth in my chest from his thoughtfulness and I smiled at him.

"I wouldn't be good company anyway because I'll probably fall asleep as soon as I get inside, but thank you for caring about me. You're a good friend, Garrett." I noticed a sudden tightening around his eyes, but then he pulled me into a tight hug.

"I do care about you and I'll always be here whenever you need me," he whispered in my ear.

"Thank you." I patted his back and started to pull away, but he held on. His hand rubbed up and down my back and I could've sworn I heard him sniff my hair, but then just as quickly as he'd pulled me in, he let me go.

"Go get some sleep before Travis starts looking into nursing homes for you," he teased, shooting me the same grin he always wore and I wondered if my sleep-deprived mind had made me imagine the odd exchange.

I flipped my middle finger at him and then opened the door and got out of the car. I could still hear him laughing as I climbed the steps and went inside. I was too tired to take the stairs, so I rode the elevator instead. I got off on the fourth floor and pulled my keys from my pocket and started to slide them in the lock, but stopped when it occurred to me that something was…off. I looked behind me and a chill swept through my body when I saw that the door across the hall was standing wide open. Even stranger was the fact that Mrs.

Stevenson was nowhere in sight.

I unlocked my door quickly and ran inside, searching for anything that could be used as a weapon then returned to the hallway. I pulled my phone from my pocket and dialed nine-one-one then let my finger hover over the send button as I crept closer to the open door. I wasn't sure what I would find inside Mrs. Stevenson's apartment so I was going to go in as prepared as possible.

For just a second, I wished that I'd let Garrett come upstairs with me, but then I realized I was being a terrible friend and that it was better that he had left so that at least one of us would survive. My heart beat wildly against my rib cage and my pulse made a loud whooshing noise in my ears. I slowly made my way inside the apartment and my eyes swept over the living room, looking for signs of foul play.

I'd always pictured Mrs. Stevenson's home to look like that of an elderly lady. Lots of antiques and trinkets that she'd collected throughout the years, but now sat collecting dust. Perhaps a cat or ten that would be lying around on every available surface and the entire place would smell like mothballs. What I saw instead was a huge surprise.

Her living room was neat and orderly with fairly modern furnishings. The place smelled like fresh baked bread and I saw no obvious signs of her having roommates of the feline variety. A sound coming from further in the apartment caught my attention and I crept slowly down the hall towards the bedroom.

The hand holding my phone shook and I glanced down to make sure the call was still ready to send then I raised my other arm as I neared the doorway. I could feel sweat trickling down my temple and I tried to swallow, but my mouth was suddenly too dry. I rounded the doorway and my eyes nearly bugged out of my head. A loud gasp escaped before I could stop it.

Morgan turned around quickly when he heard me, his own eyes widening when he saw my raised arm. I slowly lowered it, letting it drop down beside my leg. Mrs. Stevenson gave Morgan a puzzled look and then turned to see what he was staring at. Her mouth formed an O shape when she saw me standing in her doorway. The three of us stood there, staring at each other in silence until I heard a muffled voice.

"Nine-one-one, what is the nature of your emergency? Hello?" I swore under my breath as I realized that I must have hit *send* in my surprise and completed the call.

"I'm sorry, I dialed by mistake. There is no emergency," I explained quickly.

I then spent the next several minutes assuring the emergency operator that I was absolutely positive that I wasn't in any danger, followed up by a lengthy lecture on why it was important to only call nine-one-one in cases of actual emergencies. I hung up, feeling fully chastised and looked back up at the two other people in the room. Neither of them had moved from their spots, but they wore the same confused expressions on their faces.

"What the hell is going on?" I demanded.

Mrs. Stevenson's brow wrinkled and she looked up at Morgan questioningly. It wasn't until he set them down on the bed that I noticed the hammer and picture frame he'd been holding. What he did next surprised me the most out of everything that night. She smiled as he turned to her and began speaking to her, using sign language.

"I came to see you and saw your nice neighbor. We started talking and she offered me some iced tea while I waited. I noticed the picture frames she had lying on the kitchen table and offered to hang them for her. I was just getting ready to hang the last one when you showed up," Morgan explained simply.

My eyes widened even further when I saw the adoring smile

Mrs. Stevenson gave him. I raised my arm to my brow and wiped the sweat from it. I felt like I was losing my mind. Either that or I'd been so tired that I'd slipped and fallen down the stairs after Garrett dropped me off. Maybe that was it; I'd fallen, hit my head and was lying in the hospital in a coma. My parents must be so worried that I'd never wake up, I thought sadly.

"What are you doing?" Morgan asked, interrupting the devastating thoughts I was having.

"I got home and saw that Mrs. Stevenson's door was standing open and I was worried that someone had broken in. I came over to help her," I explained. Morgan tilted his head and stared down at the object in my hand then his eyes met mine.

"Let me get this straight. You thought someone had broken in and was doing something to harm your neighbor and you *brought a flyswatter*?" I noticed the slight trembling of his lips and the way his shoulders had begun to shake. I narrowed my eyes and popped my hip out, giving him my best glare, but all it did was make him howl with laughter.

I crossed my arms, the flyswatter jutting into the air as I waited for him to finish. Ten hours later, *okay maybe it was two minutes*, he settled down and began signing to Mrs. Stevenson who was looking at us strangely. I knew the moment she understood because she covered her mouth, her eyes dancing with silent laughter. I stuck my nose in the air with a sniff and rolled my eyes at both of them as Morgan began chuckling again. *She wouldn't be laughing so hard if I'd had to actually save her, and I definitely could have saved her,* I thought, soothing my bruised ego.

"Why doesn't she like me?" I hadn't even realized I'd spoken the words aloud until Morgan's head snapped up and his eyes found mine. His laughter drifted off and his eyes softened as he looked at me then he turned to face Mrs. Stevenson and signed my question to her. She turned to look at me and shook her head, then lifted her hands. Morgan acted as translator, telling me everything she said.

"She says that she does like you very much and that you've always been a nice boy, bringing her mail to her and dropping off groceries. She learned your schedule and would watch for you to make sure you made it home safely each night because you remind her of her son and she worried about you the way a mother does." Morgan smiled at that. "She was born unable to hear or speak, but most people don't bother to learn sign language so she's found that it's just easier to keep to herself."

"Why did she talk to you?" I looked at Morgan curiously.

"My charm?" Morgan suggested with a wink. I rolled my eyes even though I knew all too well how very charming the man could be. "Fine, I saw her watching me through the crack in her door and I said hello. She just stared back at me with a blank look so I decided to give signing a chance and just see what would happen. You should've seen her eyes light up when she realized I could speak to her. She invited me in and we ended up talking for over an hour. Turns out she's just a very lonely woman." My heart hurt at the thought of her being all alone, with no one to communicate with for so many years.

"You said I reminded her of her son. Where is he?" I asked. Morgan used his hands to ask Mrs. Stevenson and a happy smile spread across her face as she explained that her son had been away at a college in Europe where he'd received a full ride scholarship. When her husband died, her son had almost given up the chance because he worried about his mom, but she'd insisted he go because she didn't want him to have to take out a bunch of loans if he attended school nearby."

She smiled at both of us and then walked over to her bedside table and picked up the book that lay there. She pulled a folded piece of paper out of the book and handed it to me. I read over it and then raised my head, smiling at her. She nodded and smiled back at me.

"Her son is graduating soon and he's found a job and a place to live in France. He said there's room for her as well and that he'll fly here and get her in a few weeks," I explained to Morgan. Morgan's face split into a happy smile.

We visited with Mrs. Stevenson for a while longer and Morgan hung the last picture then we said good night. I was smiling as I stepped out of her apartment, glad to finally understand and to have made a new friend out of my neighbor.

"Thank you," I said quietly. "If it hadn't been for you, I might have never understood what was going on with her. I would've missed out on what a kind and remarkable woman she is."

"You're welcome," Morgan said with a shy smile that did strange things to my stomach. I cleared my throat.

"Why did you come here?" I asked.

"I need to know why you ran away and why you've been avoiding me," he answered bluntly. I felt my stomach drop and as tired as I was, I knew that I couldn't put him off any longer.

"Come on, we can talk in here," I told him, opening my door for him.

CHAPTER
Thirteen

Morgan

I FOLLOWED AKIO INTO HIS APARTMENT. I'D TRIED TO GIVE HIM space since it was obvious that he wasn't ready to talk to me, as evidenced by his lack of response to the numerous texts and voice messages I'd left him. I'd held out as long as I could, but after a week of not hearing from him, I just couldn't do it anymore. I enjoyed spending time with him. He made me laugh and he made me smile, he made me happy. I wasn't going to let that go without a fight.

"Would you like anything to drink?" he asked. I shook my head and he motioned for me to sit down. I chose to sit on the couch, leaving room for him next to me, but he sat in the chair instead and looked at the floor.

I let my eyes wander over him, drinking him in like a man straight out of the desert. I noticed the dark smudges under his eyes that told me he hadn't been sleeping and my hands itched to reach out and run my thumbs over the soft skin. I stared at his full bottom lip, missing the taste of him. I missed the way he felt in my arms and the smell of his skin and the sound of his laugh.

I missed Akio.

"Why did you leave?" I whispered. His eyes shot to mine and he opened his mouth, but I held my hand up, stopping him. "Don't tell me it was a work emergency either," I warned. "A work emergency wouldn't have kept you from picking up the phone or returning my texts. Something happened that made you run and I want to know what it was." He stared at me for several seconds, looking as if he were debating whether or not to answer.

"Why don't you start by explaining what that little reunion or confrontation or whatever the hell you want to call that thing between you and your ex and Bryan was all about?" Akio crossed his arms and his chin jutted out defiantly.

"Okay, I'll tell you whatever you want to know," I responded quietly. I leaned forward with my elbows on my knees and folded my hands together. Akio relaxed his arms and his face softened when he saw that I wasn't going to argue with him.

"David and I were good friends all through school, but never anything more. One night at a party, we started talking and decided to go out on a date. We had a lot of mutual interests and we had fun together so it continued and eventually we were dating exclusively. Things were good for a while, but then we started to drift apart. We'd go whole weeks where we barely said a word to each other…" I drifted off. David and I could go a week without talking and I'd been fine, but one day without Akio had me wanting to crawl out of my skin. The last week without him had been a lesson in torture. The meaning behind that was not lost on me.

"So you two just drifted apart?" I looked at Akio and saw the doubt in his eyes. He knew there was more to it than that.

"Not exactly," I said. "We both realized that things were starting to slip away so we decided to move in together. You know, the whole out of sight, out of mind thing? I guess we figured that if we lived together then the opposite would happen and we'd be forced to interact, but instead, the distance became even more glaringly obvious. I thought that no matter what, we would always be friends though. It never even occurred to me…" I shook my head.

"We'd both been really busy, my best friend and foreman, Bryan, had been calling off work a lot and I'd had to cover both of our jobs." Akio's eyes widened at the mention of Bryan's name, but he remained quiet, letting me tell the story in my own way. "I managed to get away a little early one day and I went home with the plans to spend some time with David, maybe take him out to dinner. He was in the shower when I got there, but when I opened the door, I realized he wasn't alone and to make matters worse, he was in there with Bryan."

"Oh shit!" I heard Akio gasp. His face was a mixture of sympathy and horror and God, I loved him even more for it.

"Yeah, I thought they were my friends, but it turns out they'd been seeing each other behind my back," I explained. It was funny how their betrayal didn't carry the same weight since Akio had come into my life. It was as if the light that shone from him had banished out all the shadows of my past and made them hurt less. I rolled my eyes at the direction of my thoughts. When had I turned into a teenage girl?

"I'm sorry they did that to you, no one deserves that. It explains a lot though," Akio said quietly.

"How so?" I asked, tilting my head at him. His eyes moved to the floor, avoiding my gaze.

"You'd been trying to work things out with David and he meant a great deal to you. It had to hurt very badly to see him with your best friend, of all people. You want him back and then to see him still with Bryan when we ran into them in town, no wonder you were so upset." My jaw dropped open, but Akio continued before I could say anything.

"Where did I fit into all of this?" he asked quietly. "Was I just the rebound guy? Someone to help you pass the time until you could get David back?" I heard the resignation in his voice and my vision went fuzzy. How could he even think that?

"No!" I shouted. Akio's head shot up at my sudden outburst. "No, Akio, you've got it completely wrong. I don't want David back, he and I were all wrong for each other. I figured out a long time ago that he and I should have never tried to be more than friends. That was never more glaringly obvious than when I saw him in the shower with Bryan and I realized that I was more upset about being lied to by two people I trusted than the fact that our relationship was over. I was upset when we saw them that day, but not because they were together; I was upset because I didn't want them touching you. I didn't want the ugly part of my past to be anywhere near you." My heart was racing with what I was about to say, but I drew in a deep breath and continued.

"I figured something in me was broken because it hadn't hurt as much as I thought it should when David and I broke up. I assumed maybe I just didn't feel things as deeply as other people did, but Landon told me that it was just because I hadn't met the right person yet." I let out a small laugh and shook my head. "I told him I wasn't sure there was someone out there for me, but I was wrong." I stared directly into Akio's eyes to make sure he was listening and would hear my next words.

"I knew I was wrong as soon as I began spending time with you. Things with David were comfortable and easy, but when I'm with you, I feel like I'm on the most exhilarating roller coaster. There's that intense chemistry between us, I know you've felt it too, but it's more than that. I feel happier and more complete when I'm with you. You make me think about the future and dream about things that I used to never think were possible." His eyes widened and I could see cautious hopefulness staring back at me.

"Then why didn't you open the door?" he whispered.

"What?" I looked at him in confusion, trying to make sense of his words.

"After we ran into David and Bryan, I knew you were upset, but you left me standing there on the sidewalk while you climbed into your truck and you never opened my door. Then you did it again when we got to the cabin. You just got right out and never came to open my door for me," he explained and I hated the way his voice shook.

"I told you before that the guys I've dated have never treated me like an equal. They've always seen me as someone who needed to be taken care of, but could never help take care of them. Most just saw me as a good time, someone they could play with until the right guy came along. Then you came along and you opened doors for me." The awe in his voice made my heart hurt.

"I know it probably sounds crazy and that to most people it's a very minor thing, but to me, opening my doors meant that I was special, that I was important. It was a way of saying that I was worth the extra time and effort it took to make that gesture. I didn't realize how much I'd grown accustomed to it, until it was gone and then I felt unimportant. Coupled with the fact that it all happened after you saw your ex and I felt like the same thing that had happened with all those other guys was about to happen again."

"Is that why you took off and wouldn't talk to me this past week?" I asked incredulously.

"I know it probably doesn't make any sense to you, but yes. I left because I had to protect myself. The other men hurt me when they treated me that way, but it was nothing compared to what you could…" Akio trailed off, stopping himself from finishing what he was going to say. I stood up and went over to his chair then knelt in front of him. I reached for his hands and was grateful when he didn't pull away.

"I am so sorry that I hurt you, I had no idea what opening the door meant to you. I promise that I will never let anything distract me again from making you feel like the most important person in the world to me because you are. I love you. I'm completely *in* love with you. You could never just be a rebound or someone to help pass the time. Akio, to me, you're the main event."

Akio looked at me then in a way that I would carry in my heart forever. It was a look filled with wonder and hope, happiness and completeness; all the things I felt when I looked at him.

"I'm in love with you too, Morgan. I have been for a long time," he whispered.

I leaned forward then and cupping his face in my hands, pulled him towards me for a kiss. Our hearts spoke to each other in that kiss, things that we could never express with mere words and I finally understood what my cousins had told me about finding your soulmate. They'd said it felt like you'd finally found the other half of yourself and that's exactly how I felt about Akio.

I woke the next morning and smiled when I saw Akio. He looked like a starfish with the way he was sprawled out next to me in the bed. He'd barely been able to keep his eyes open after our talk the night before so I'd sent him to bed while I'd walked through his apartment, turning off the lights and making sure the door was locked. He'd already started to doze when I crawled into bed beside him, but he woke up long enough to curl his body around mine and whisper that he loved me before he drifted off.

I could understand his exhaustion because I hadn't slept very well the week before either, but lying in his bed with his warm body pressed to mine and the knowledge that he loved me as much as I loved him, I was able to sleep better than I could ever remember.

I took advantage of the fact that he was sleeping soundly to let my eyes wander leisurely over his tight little body. His silky black hair which lay messily in all directions was in direct contrast to the crisp white pillowcase beneath his head. His long lashes were fanned out over his delicate cheekbones and his full lips begged to be kissed.

His chest rose and fell with his even breathing and I longed to trace the flat brown discs of his nipples with my tongue. I could see the firm muscles of his abs, not protruding from his body, but lying just under the surface of his skin like a quiet strength. The sheets had made their way down to his waist and he had one knee curved out from under the covers. My mouth watered as I pictured what he had hidden right below the thin material.

I moved slowly, carefully lifting the sheet to reveal his cock that was half hard and resting against his thigh. I kept my eyes on his face as I lowered my head and took him in my mouth. His eyes sprung open with a gasp and I chuckled around my morning treat.

"Good morning, baby," I whispered and then flattened my tongue and swiped it up the length of his shaft.

Akio smiled at me with those big brown eyes so full of love even in their sleepiness and my heart skipped a beat. I wondered if he had any idea the kind of power he had over me. I swirled my tongue over the head of his dick and then sucked him into my mouth, feeling him harden and lengthen until the tip was snuggled deep inside my throat. I moaned at the taste of him and his hips shot off the bed as my mouth vibrated around him. I bobbed my head up and down, alternating between sucking and tonguing him until I felt his hands pushing my head away.

"I want you to come down my throat," I complained and he made that sound I loved, the one that sounded like the mewl of a kitten.

"I want that too, trust me," he said, surprising me by sitting up. "But you're not the only one who's hungry. Lie down," he ordered and I scurried back up the bed with a smile on my face.

I rolled onto my back and Akio threw his leg over me, straddling me in a sixty-nine position. I felt his lips on the inside of my thigh and I reached up and bit one of his firm ass cheeks. He retaliated by sucking one of my balls into his warm, wet mouth and swirling it around with his tongue and from that moment, it was game on; each one of us trying to outdo the other as we raced towards the finish line.

I could feel my dick being sucked down into the tight constraints of his throat and when he swallowed around me, I had to fight to keep from exploding. I wanted to hold off as long as possible because I wanted to come with him. I wasn't sure why, maybe it was left over emotions from the night before or having spent the last week without him, but it was important to me that we share that moment together.

I knew I wouldn't be able to hold out forever though, especially with Akio's talented mouth, so I doubled my efforts on him. I stuck a finger into my mouth, wetting it, then used it to circle his pretty hole. His hips bucked back, seeking more so I slid my finger inside his tight channel at the same time I sucked his cock into my mouth. He moaned loudly and laid his forehead against the inside of my leg, his hot breath hitting me as he panted.

I slid my finger in and out, coaxing him open and shivered when I was rewarded with a burst of pre-cum which I drank right down. I was thirsty for more and I couldn't wait for him to shoot down my throat. The room filled with the sounds of slurping and moaning as we worked each other into a frenzy.

The dual sensation of his taste on my tongue and his lips around my cock had me hovering on the edge, so I sucked him harder and slid my finger further inside him, crooking it at just the right spot. Akio stiffened above me and salty goodness filled my throat at the same time I spilled over into his waiting mouth. We continued sucking and licking each other clean until every last drop was gone and the tremors had finished wracking our bodies then he climbed off of me and turned, laying his head on my shoulder.

"Good morning," he whispered and I chuckled at the satisfied grin on his face.

"Good morning," I whispered back, bending my head for a kiss.

"I love you."

"So, I didn't dream that part?" he asked, his eyes sparkling with happiness.

"No, baby. That part is all real and it's never going to change," I assured him.

"Good, because I love you too." Akio leaned up for one more kiss and then laid his head back on my shoulder and began tracing patterns across my chest. I sighed contentedly, enjoying the feel of him in my arms. It was so quiet that I would've thought he'd fallen back asleep if it weren't for his finger still moving over my skin.

"Do you have any plans today?" I asked.

"No, why?" Akio shifted his body so he could look at me and folded his hands over my chest, resting his chin on them.

"I want to spend the day with you and I have something to show you," I said, sifting my fingers through his hair.

"The last time you had something to show me, we ended up having sex in the back of your truck," he teased, wiggling his brows at me. My cock stirred in response to the memory.

"Are you complaining?" I asked, lowering my voice in the way I knew drove him crazy. It worked because he wriggled his hips against the bed.

"Not at all," he answered then laughed as I flipped us over so he lay pinned under me.

"Let's get a shower so we can get going then," I told him, pressing my lips to his. We were both breathless when we ended the kiss.

"Wait, I was kind of hoping the thing you wanted to show me was in this bed," he whined playfully. "You know, kind of like that thing you do with your tongue and my ass…"

"If you get in that shower right now, I'll show you that thing I do with my hand on your ass," I promised.

"Get off of me, you big oaf, I have an appointment with my shower," he joked, pushing on my chest and rolling out from under me.

"Big oaf?" I sputtered. "That's it, you're getting more than one spanking."

"Promises, promises," Akio yelled over his shoulder then shrieked loudly when he saw me jump out of bed and start chasing him down the hallway to the bathroom.

This…this is what I have been waiting all my life to find, I thought as I caught up to him and wrapped my arms around his waist, silencing his laughs with a kiss. I'd finally found it and I wasn't ever going to let it go.

CHAPTER
Fourteen

Morgan

I PULLED INTO THE PARKING LOT AND SMILED AS I LOOKED AT THE non-descript gray building in front of me. I'd been considering what I was about to do for a long time and finally made the decision to go for it. I turned to look at Akio who was staring at the front of the building with his face scrunched up in confusion. The look was adorable on him and when he turned his head towards me, I couldn't resist leaning over to kiss the tip of his nose.

"You wanted to show me an animal shelter?" he asked.

"No, this is just a stop along the way," I explained.

"Do you come here often?" I laughed and Akio rolled his eyes as he realized how his question had sounded.

"No wonder you needed Curtis to set you up if that's the kind of pick-up lines you usually use," I teased. I watched in amusement as his diva side presented itself. I loved his diva side. In fact, I hadn't seen a side of Akio I didn't like.

"Boy, if I remember correctly, all I needed to do was show up at work and you were ready to date me," he replied, crossing his arms and swiveling his head at me.

"That is very true. One look at you and I was hooked," I admitted, moving in close enough to brush his lips with mine. I kissed my way across his jaw until I reached his ear and then I bit gently at his lobe, making him shiver.

"If you want me to go in there with you then you better stop," he said breathlessly. I glanced down at the bulge forming in his pants and smiled proudly. I loved the way his body responded to me so easily.

"Fine, I'll be good, but only until I get you alone again," I promised. Akio mumbled something under his breath that sounded like "counting on it," but I couldn't be sure.

"What are we doing here?" he asked as we got out and started walking towards the shelter. I reached down and took his hand. He glanced at it and then smiled back at me.

"I've been thinking about getting another dog for a while," I told him. "Carly is the best dog and she was my best friend, growing up. She went everywhere with me, always keeping me company since I didn't have any sisters or brothers to play with. You saw her though, she's old and it's hard for her to get around. There was no way I could bring her with me when I moved. It would've been too hard for her to adjust, plus Mom and Dad love her so I didn't want to take her away from them."

"So, what kind of dog are you wanting to get?" Akio asked.

"I actually already found a few, but I need your help deciding which one," I answered as I held the front door open for him. His eyes flickered to mine and he wore a small smile as he passed.

Having already called to tell them I was coming, all I had to do was give my name to the woman at the front desk and she led us to a back hallway. There were rooms on either side that had large windows so you could easily look inside. We passed several rooms that held dogs and cats in all varieties and colors. The place was kept very clean and I could see many toys and climbers for the animals to enjoy. Finally, the woman stopped and turned to us with a bright smile.

"They're in here. This is a big decision so feel free to take your time. I'll leave you alone to get to know them, but you come get me if you have any questions or once you've decided."

I thanked her and then we went inside. My heart melted as soon as I saw the little balls of fluff that came charging at us. I'd been watching the shelter's online site for weeks, looking for just the right dog. I knew that whatever I chose would have to be special. After all, it had pretty big shoes to fill if it were going to try to follow up Carly.

The day before, I'd finally found what I was looking for. A litter of golden retriever puppies had been left in a box on the side of the road and someone had found them and brought them to the shelter. There were six in all, two boys and four girls. They'd warned me when I'd called that they would be adopted quickly so I immediately set up a time for me to see them. I laughed as they tugged at my shoelaces and chewed on each other's ears.

I turned to see what Akio thought and was surprised to find him sitting cross-legged on the floor. He was holding a puppy up to his face and laughed when it stuck it's tongue out and licked his chin. I got down on the floor beside him and smiled at the pure joy on his face. Several of the puppies climbed into our laps.

"How are we supposed to choose just one?" he asked, looking at me with a helpless grin.

It took a while, but finally, we were able to pick just one. I curled an arm around Akio as we left the room, reassuring him that they would all find good homes when I saw the concerned expression on his face. Thankfully, the woman who'd helped us before told him the same thing and he was smiling again by the time we left.

"Where to now?" Akio asked as he buckled his seatbelt.

"The pet store is next so we can get some supplies for this little girl and then I want to show you my home," I replied, handing the puppy back to him.

"Thank you for including me in this and for taking me to see your house," he said quietly.

"I love you and I want you to be a part of my life, Akio," I told him. I saw the happiness, but also a bit of uncertainty in his eyes as he looked at me. I hated the fact that he'd been hurt enough that he felt that he had to be cautious, but I was determined to prove to him that I wanted him in my life and not just for the moment. I wanted him there as long as possible, for the rest of my life if I had any say in the matter.

I started the truck and looked over at him again as he nuzzled his face against Angel's soft furry ears. He caught my gaze and smiled back at me. *Does life get any better than this?*

I set Angel down on the grass and let her explore and began pulling the pet store supplies from the back of the truck. Akio turned in a circle, taking in the cabin and the rest of the property that made up my home.

"This is amazing, Morgan," he exclaimed and I smiled, pleased that he approved.

"Thank you. Come on, I want to show you inside." I carried the small kennel I'd bought as well as the fluffy pink dog bed, that Akio insisted every princess pup should have, into the cabin and set them down then froze when I heard Akio talking to Angel in a cutsie little voice.

"Who went wee in the grass? Angel did. That's right. You sure did because you're a good doggy, aren't you? Yes, you are. Oh, yes you are." His head shot up when I started laughing and the startled expression on his face told me that he'd forgotten I was even there.

"If you're all finished embarrassing the dog, I'll show you around," I teased.

"I wasn't embarrassing her," he huffed.

"All I know is she rolled her eyes and gave me a look that begged for help," I stated, holding my hands up in surrender.

"Are you jealous?" Akio teased, narrowing his eyes at me.

"Me? Jealous? Why would I be jealous? Just because you've spent the morning kissing her and rubbing her and whispering things to her," I pouted playfully. He walked towards me and the seductive grin on his face had me wanting to rip his clothes off and bury myself in his tight warmth.

"Don't worry, sugar, I plan on spending the entire night doing the same things to you, only more." He chuckled as I reached down to adjust myself, proud of himself for turning the tables on me. I'd let him have that one, but only because I was envisioning the way his ass would look later that night, all red with my handprints and warm to the touch.

I showed Akio around the cabin and then took him out to my workshop. I felt strangely nervous as he stepped inside and looked around, but I suppose it made sense. I'd never let anyone else into my private sanctuary before and it felt like I was leaving myself vulnerable, but then he turned and smiled and it was as if something settled inside me and I smiled back. It felt right to have him there.

"Did you make this?" he asked as he wandered over to the table I'd finished making right before we'd left for the wedding.

"Yeah, it just needs to be sanded down and stained and then it'll be finished," I told him.

"It's beautiful," he praised and then moved around the room, checking out the other pieces of furniture I'd made. "You are really talented. Have you ever thought of doing that for a living? There are a lot of people who would pay top dollar to have custom pieces built."

"Nah, I just like doing it in my spare time. It relaxes me and gives me a chance to build something just for fun with no deadline," I said and he nodded his head in understanding.

"Well, I think it's amazing. Thank you for showing me," he said sincerely.

"You're welcome," I mumbled, suddenly feeling shy.

We took a walk through the woods after that, holding hands along the way and stopping to make out against a large oak tree. It occurred to me as we walked back to the house that that was the first time since I'd moved in that my place had felt like home to me and I knew it was because of the man walking beside me.

We took Angel outside and let her play in the yard while we sat on the front porch steps, talking and drinking lemonade. It had been a perfect day and I found myself wishing it would never end. I'd just opened my mouth to tell Akio that, but was cut off by the sound of his phone ringing. I watched him curiously as he pulled it from his pocket and smiled down at the screen before answering it.

"Hey, Mom. How are you?" He caught my stare and I smiled at him. "Hang on a minute, Mom," he said after a few seconds of listening to her. He covered the phone with his hand and gave me an apologetic look. "I haven't seen my parents since before the wedding and they want me to come over for dinner."

"Oh, that's fine. Of course, you should go," I told him, trying to hide my disappointment. It was his parents and I completely understood that he needed to spend time with them, I just hated seeing him leave after spending such a wonderful day with him.

"Are you sure? If you had other plans, we don't have to go over there," he said, watching my reaction closely.

"We?" I asked in surprise.

"Yes, we. Did you think I was going to leave you here?" He sounded like the idea was completely ridiculous.

"No," I scoffed. I shrugged my shoulders, not wanting to admit that that was exactly what I'd thought was going to happen. His forehead scrunched as he looked at me and I could tell he wasn't buying it. He held his phone back up to his ear.

"Yeah, Mom, I'll be there for dinner…and I'm bringing someone with me that I'd like you to meet." He was quiet for a minute while his mom spoke and I wished I could hear what she was saying. "Yeah, he is," Akio answered quietly and then held his phone away from his ear as a loud shriek rang out. He was laughing as he finished speaking to her. When he hung up, I looked at him questioningly.

"She wanted to know if the person I was bringing home was someone special," he admitted, scooting closer and laying his head on my shoulder. I wrapped my arm around his waist and kissed the top of his head.

"What did you tell her?" I asked, a wide smile splitting my face.

"You heard what I told her," he said, tilting his head to look up at me.

"Maybe I want to hear it again," I whispered.

"Maybe I should show you instead," he whispered back, his warm breath ghosting across my face and causing me to shiver. Our lips met in a slow, sweet kiss. Yes, it had been a perfect day so far.

"Oh no!" Akio groaned.

"What's wrong?" I asked as I pulled into the driveway of his parents' house.

"Dad's grilling," he answered darkly. I pulled to a stop and looked at him curiously.

"Is that a bad thing? And how do you know he's grilling when we just pulled in?" He pointed out the window instead of answering. I followed the direction of his finger and saw a dark plume of smoke billowing up from the direction of the backyard.

"Oh!" I breathed out as both questions were answered at once.

"Oh, is right!" he sighed. "Dad can't grill, at all. The problem is, he doesn't know it and Mom and I don't have the heart to tell him because he enjoys it so much."

"I think it's incredibly sweet that you've suffered through years of charred meat just so you won't hurt your dad's feelings. Don't worry though, he won't hear it from me," I assured him.

"Thanks. Just do what Mom and I do and use lots of ketchup," he suggested. I laughed as he shook his head woefully.

"So, do your parents know anything about me, other than the fact that you're bringing someone with you for dinner?" I was holding his hand as we started up the front steps.

"I may have talked about you a little," he answered vaguely as the front door swung open and we were greeted by a tiny woman, even shorter than Akio with the same beautiful brown eyes as her son and a pleasant smile.

"Musuko!" she exclaimed happily as she wrapped her arms around his waist.

"Hey, Mom," Akio said with a smile, wrapping his arms around her and hugging her back. He stepped back after a couple of seconds. "There's someone I want you to meet. Mom, this is Morgan."

"Hello, ma'am. I'm Morgan Greene, it's nice to meet you." I started to extend my hand, but she brushed it aside as she grabbed me in a strong hug, much stronger than I'd expected from such a small woman.

"Please, call me Rena. It's so nice to finally meet you. Akio has been going on and on about you," she gushed.

"Oh, he has, has he?" I said, smirking at Akio over his mom's head. He rolled his eyes, but I could see the pink tint to his cheeks. It made me happy to know that he'd been talking about me with the people he was closest to.

"Well, come on in, boys. Your dad is out back...grilling." Rena rolled her eyes and making us both laugh.

"We saw the smoke when we pulled up. We'll go outside and say hello, you get the ketchup ready," Akio joked.

"Already on the table," she informed him dryly.

"Hey, Dad! How's it going?" Akio said as we stepped out onto the back deck.

His father looked up from where he was standing and my eyes widened. He was wearing an apron with an image of a male body builder on the front and was holding a pair of long, metal tongs. Dark puffs of smoke were leaking out the sides of the grill where a tray of meat sat.

I'd pictured Akio's dad to be shorter and not frail, but definitely on the thin side. What I saw however, was the exact opposite. He was a handsome man, around my height with broad shoulders, and large muscular arms. He had thick salt and pepper hair, blue eyes, and a friendly smile which he bestowed upon his only child as soon as he heard his voice. I liked him immediately.

"Akio! How are you, son?" he called out. His eyes shifted over to me and his smile grew even wider. "Rena told me you were bringing someone special with you." I chuckled as Akio cursed under his breath.

"Thanks, Dad, I appreciate that," Akio said sarcastically. "This is Morgan Greene. Morgan, my father, Henry."

"Hello! It's nice to meet you, sir," I said, shaking his hand.

"Nice to meet you too, Morgan, and call me Henry."

"How much meat are you grilling, Dad? It's just the four of us, isn't it?" Akio asked, his eyes darting back and forth between the tray of meat and the closed lid of the grill.

"Oh, that's not meat under there. I'm trying this thing I saw on TV where you wrap the vegetables and potatoes up in foil and grill them. That's what's on right now," he explained and he looked so happy that I could understand why Akio and his mother wouldn't want to hurt him by complaining.

Right then, Rena called Akio in to help her with something in the kitchen. He looked at me nervously, but I motioned for him to go on, I'd be fine out there with his father. I watched him walk inside and was smiling when I turned to face Henry who was staring at me with his head cocked to the side and a look of concentration on his face.

"I hope I didn't embarrass you by what I said earlier," he said slowly.

"About Akio bringing someone special?" I asked. Henry nodded. "Not at all. In fact, it makes me very happy. Akio and I already know how we feel about each other, but it's nice to know he's talked about me with you and your wife. I know how close you are."

"We are close. Akio is a good boy, always has been. He's thoughtful and caring, almost to a fault because it's led to him getting his heart stomped on more than a few times." I winced at the thought of Akio in pain. "He's learned to be cautious, but when he loves someone, he loves with his whole heart. I may be biased since I'm his dad, but whoever ends up with my boy is going to be a damn lucky man and he better treat him with all the love and respect he deserves." I could tell how serious he was so my response was honest and sincere.

"I love your son very much, Henry. It breaks my heart that anyone could have ever treated him poorly because I know how very special he is. I promise you that his heart is safe with me," I told him. Seconds felt like hours as he stared at me, but then a slow smile spread across his face and he nodded.

"Good," was all he said and then he turned his attention back to the grill. "I imagine the vegetables are probably about done, don't you think?" he asked as he lifted the grill lid. I stared down at the charred remains of the foil and tried to keep my horror from showing on my face.

"I think so," I agreed. "Would you mind if I help with the meat? I used to grill all the time back home, but I haven't bought a new one yet and I miss it."

"You're a grilling man?" Henry asked, his entire face lighting up like a kid's on Christmas morning. "I think we're going to get along just fine," he announced as he slapped me on the back.

Akio and his mom came out carrying bowls of food which they set on the picnic table. Akio gave me a questioning look and I knew he was worried about what his dad might have said to me. I gave him a reassuring smile and I watched as his shoulders relaxed then I turned back to Henry and began grilling.

CHAPTER
Fifteen

Akio

IT HAD BEEN OVER A MONTH SINCE MORGAN AND I HAD admitted our feelings to each other and I could honestly say that I'd never been happier. He and my dad had hit it off that night and my mom adored him. Of course, I'm not sure how much of that was because he made me happy or because he'd actually taught my dad how to grill properly. Either way, she looked at Morgan like he hung the moon, *not all that different from how I look at him*, I thought with a smile.

Morgan and I helped Mrs. Stevenson pack up her things and when her son came to pick her up, we took them out to dinner so we could get to know him. He promised to take good care of her and she and I promised to keep in touch through texting which I had taught her to do. It seemed strange and a little lonely without her in the building and I realized how much I'd always counted on her presence in the hallway when I got home each night.

Soon after, I started spending nearly every night at Morgan's place. I told him it was because I wanted to be with Angel, but the truth was that it had very quickly begun to feel like home to me. That scared me a little because even though a day hadn't gone by without Morgan telling me or showing me how much he loved me, there was still that niggling doubt that one day he'd tire of me and walk away. It wasn't that I doubted him or his words, it was just that I doubted my ability to hold his attention. I didn't say anything to him about it, but Morgan had a way of reading my mind and he told me that he thought I was the most amazing and interesting person he'd ever known and that he wasn't going anywhere. And then he'd proceeded to prove just how much he loved me in many different ways and for many hours.

Landon had gotten back from his honeymoon with Micah and stopped in to see how things were going with the Agape House project. He was very impressed with the progress being made and the quality of Morgan's work, although he said he wasn't surprised in the least. He knew his cousin would be the right man for the job all along.

I finished typing up the email I'd been working on and hit send then checked the time on my watch. If I left right then, I'd have just enough time to get to Morgan's for a quick shower before we needed to head out again. Hopefully Morgan wasn't running late on his end.

Kathy Greene had been chosen by the group to oversee a fundraiser that would get the community involved in the project while bringing awareness to what Agape House was all about and what they were offering the youth of Chicago. She'd chosen to do a carnival in the hopes that it would attract families and young couples who might be more willing to donate their time to the project. As soon as it was announced that Carter's Creed had offered to put on a small concert, tickets started selling like crazy. Whether people were coming for the concert or just to have fun at the carnival, it didn't matter. The most important thing was getting the community more involved in such a worthwhile cause. I climbed in my car just as my phone rang. My heart flipped and I smiled when I saw it was Morgan.

"Hey, sexy man, I was just thinking about you," I said in greeting.

"You were, were you? Do I get to hear these thoughts?" he asked. I pulled out onto the street as I continued to talk.

"It involved you and me," I teased.

"Tell me more," he demanded, his voice lowering an octave. My blood immediately rushed to my cock, making it hard and I was thankful that I was in my car instead of my office.

"Well, we were in your shower and I'd just finished lathering you up. You had soap bubbles gliding across your chest, down over those washboard abs I love so much and pooling into the dark hair around your thick cock." I heard a loud groan through the phone and I felt a trickle of sweat run down my back.

"The spray of the water rinsed you off and my knees hit the floor of the shower. I lifted your heavy cock in my hand and flicked my tongue over it, tasting you and then I reached down and began stroking myself as I sucked you down my throat."

"Stop," Morgan hissed. "Get home right now. I'm pulling in the driveway and I'll be waiting for you in the shower." He hung up before I could respond and I smiled. I loved getting him all worked up, knowing that I was the only one that would reap the benefits of it. I also hadn't missed the fact that he'd told me to come home. Not his place, but home. My heart fluttered with the hope that it actually would be my home one day.

We arrived at the carnival a little late. Okay, a lot late, but my man had been insatiable after our conversation and he'd made good on everything I'd described and then some. Morgan had smirked when I came out of his bedroom after getting dressed and he noticed I was walking a little differently than normal. I'd rolled my eyes at him, but he'd just smiled proudly and told me that I'd have no choice but to think of him all night. I assured him that I was always thinking about him, even when I was supposed to be working. He told me that he did the same which led to another make out session which led to another round of orgasms.

I'd been tempted to stay home and continue our night in the same fashion, but then I remembered what the carnival would mean to the kids of Agape House and also that I'd invited my friends to come. Travis, Garrett, and Jasper were important to me and I was anxious for them to meet Morgan.

Several city blocks had been shut off for the use of the carnival and Micah had arranged a large team of security to watch over the band as well as his friends and family members. Some might think he went a little overboard on his protectiveness, but given everything he'd been through in the military as well as nearly losing Landon, I could understand why it would make him feel better to know that he had people watching over those he cared about the most.

Caleb and Giovanni were the first familiar faces we saw and we stopped to talk to them. They were there with their daughter, Sarah, who had a butterfly painted on her face. Giovanni was holding her in his arms and she squealed with delight every time he'd pretend to snatch a bite of the cotton candy she was holding.

I watched as Morgan quietly asked her for a bite and she handed him a sticky fistful. She grinned at him as he ate it and the look on her face said that she was as charmed by him as I was. I got lost in my thoughts about how good he was with her and what an amazing father he would be when I felt someone staring at me. Caleb was watching me with a knowing smile and I blushed when I realized he'd read my thoughts, but then he winked at me and pulled a pouch of wet wipes out of the bag around his shoulder, offering one to Giovanni and another one to Morgan. The men wiped the stickiness from their faces while Caleb set to work cleaning Sarah. They moved on when Sarah saw the merry-go-round and Morgan leaned down to whisper in my ear, his breath sweet from the cotton candy.

"I want one…or three of those someday. Of course, I want to do things right. I need to put a ring on your finger and get you down the aisle before we start working on having little Akios running around."

He leaned back so he could gauge my reaction and frowned at what I'm sure was a stunned expression on my face. That was the first time either of us had really talked about our future together, but warmth spread over my body at the thought of spending the rest of my life with Morgan and I knew that there was nothing I wanted more. I reached up and wrapped my arms around his neck and I felt him relax as he lowered his forehead to mine, his arms sliding around my waist.

"I want that too. So much," I whispered and I could feel his smile as his lips pressed to mine.

I wasn't sure how long we stood there with our arms around each other, the sounds of the nearby carnival games and children laughing as they rode the rides growing more distant the longer we kissed, completely lost in each other. It wasn't until I heard a throat clearing directly behind me that I pulled away from him and turned in his arms. Travis and Jasper stood there with matching grins and I wondered how long they'd been standing there. I noticed Garrett a few steps behind them, his face unreadable.

"Hey, guys! Sorry, I didn't see you walking up," I told them, feeling my face flush from embarrassment. Either that, or the heat of Morgan's kiss, it really could be both.

"We noticed," Travis teased. "So, you must be the stud muffin we've heard so much about. I'm Travis," he said, thrusting his hand out for Morgan to shake and ignoring the glare I was shooting at him. I should have known I could count on Travis to embarrass me.

"Morgan Greene, and it's good to know what Akio's been calling me," Morgan said without missing a beat as he reached around my waist to shake Travis's hand.

"I'm going to start calling you both some new names if you don't knock it off," I threatened, but I only succeeded in making them laugh harder. I made a mental note to keep the two of them far apart for my own sanity.

"Hi, I'm Jasper," Jasper introduced himself quietly as he offered his hand. Morgan took it and told him it was nice to meet him. I smiled happily. It was nice to finally have my friends getting to know the man in my life.

"And that's Garrett in the back. Get up here, Garrett," I said, smiling at my friend. He didn't smile back which was unlike him, but he stepped forward and offered his hand to Morgan.

"It's nice to meet you too," Morgan said, and Garrett mumbled a response.

Their handshake lasted longer than the others and I glanced down to see Garrett's fingers turn white. My eyes shot to his face, but he let go right then and took a step back. I looked over my shoulder at Morgan and saw the hard look in his eyes as he continued to stare at Garrett. The entire exchange only lasted a few seconds, but it left me feeling confused.

We all walked around for a while, playing a few games and having fun. I was happy to see Travis, Jasper, and Morgan getting along, but I noticed that Garrett hung back from the rest of us. I slowed my pace until he caught up with me and then walked beside him, the others laughing up ahead. I tried to make small talk with him about the carnival, but he only gave me short, one-word responses. Something was clearly bothering him and I wanted to know what it was in case it was something I could help with. Garrett had always been there for me and I wanted to do the same for him.

"Are you okay?" I asked quietly. If it was something he didn't want shared with the rest of the group then I didn't want to call attention to it. His head shot over to look at me and then his forehead wrinkled in confusion.

"I just don't get it. You and Morgan?" he whispered.

"What do you mean?" I asked, confusion clear in my voice.

"I mean that last time we talked he had upset you and you said it was over." Garrett frowned down at me and I felt my back straighten defensively.

"We talked and were able to work things out. Why are you getting upset about it?" I asked.

"I'm not upset about it, Akio. I want you to be happy; that's all I've ever wanted. I just thought…" Garrett's voice drifted off and he let out a long sigh. I still didn't understand what was bothering him, but I hated seeing my friend upset.

"Look, Garrett, what happened between me and Morgan before was a misunderstanding and we were able to work through it. He's a great guy and I think if you got to know him, you'd see that," I said. I laid my hand on his arm and he stared down at it then glanced back up at me, his eyes searching mine for…something, I wasn't sure what.

"I know I've been really busy lately, but you're still my friend and I'm here if you ever want to talk, okay?" I smiled at him and waited until he nodded and smiled back. We continued walking together and talking, nothing heavy, just catching up with each other until Travis complained he was starving so the three of them took off in search of food while Morgan and I headed towards the concert area.

"Everything okay with your friend?" he asked gently.

"I guess so, I'm not really sure what's going on with him," I answered.

"I have a pretty good idea," Morgan muttered darkly.

I narrowed my eyes in question, but someone called my name before I could ask him what he'd meant. We turned our heads and saw Lachlan Edwards making his way through the crowd, a large security guard at his side. Several people turned their heads as he walked by and I wasn't sure if it was because they recognized him from having his face splashed on the covers of all the rag magazines ever since he got engaged to Rylie, the drummer of Carter's Creed, or if it was because he was just *that* good looking. He gave us each a hug when he reached us.

"How are you guys? I haven't seen you since Micah and Landon's wedding," he said in a smooth British accent.

"We're good. How are you and Rylie?" I asked. Lachlan's face split into a wide smile when I mentioned his fiancé.

"We're very well, thank you. We've been preparing for our own wedding," he said.

"Yes, we got our invitations this week. We're looking forward to it," I told him.

"That's wonderful. It's very important to each of us to have our closest friends there because you all have become our family," Lachlan explained and I was even more touched to be included in their special day. I assured him that we wouldn't miss it for the world and then he excused himself to go check on the band and see if there was anything they needed before their performance.

Landon and Micah walked up then and they had Matt and Isaac with them. Landon smiled when he saw our joined hands. Morgan and I had already told him that we were together once he got back from his honeymoon, but he still looked so happy about it whenever he saw us together. I knew that he'd been worried about me for a long time and he was equally concerned when Morgan had broken up with David. Landon had always been a caretaker, a nurturer to those he cared about so I knew it had brought him peace of mind to known that Morgan and I had found each other.

"Can you believe this turnout?" Matt asked incredulously. His head turned as he took in the crowd that had gathered for the concert as well as the people lining the streets for the carnival.

"It's a very good thing for Agape House to have this much awareness brought to it," I said.

"How is the project going?" Matt turned his attention to Morgan. We all listened as Morgan described the progress so far and everyone was excited to hear that he was way ahead of schedule. I was so proud of him and the work that he'd done in such a short amount of time.

We turned our attention to the stage as the concert began. Carter was at his best, working the crowd into a frenzy and turning most of the audience into putty in his hands. He was incredibly talented, as was the rest of the band. Rylie looked healthy and strong behind his drum set and most people would be surprised to find out how close we'd come to losing him.

Carter slowed the music down and the crowd let out a loud "Awww!" as he dedicated the next song to his husband, Ryan. Whistles and shouts of "CRYAN!" could be heard as the band started playing the beginning notes of "One Call Away."

The rest of the Greene family had joined us by then and I smiled as I looked around at all my friends and family. A few were kissing, some were smiling or singing along and a couple were even swaying together in a slow dance. Morgan pulled me back against his chest and wrapped his arms around me. Then his lips brushed over my ear and he whispered what he was going to do to me later and everything and everyone else around me was forgotten.

CHAPTER
Sixteen

Morgan

"OKAY, MOM, I'VE GOT TO GO. I LOVE YOU TOO." I HUNG up the phone and glared down at Akio who was grinning up at me innocently from between my legs.

"I can't believe you did that while I was on the phone with my mother," I growled.

"I can't believe you managed to speak through that. I must be losing my touch." He was laughing as I pulled him up and flipped us so that he was underneath me, my forearms resting on either side of his head.

"I had to tell her I'd just gotten back from a run so she wouldn't wonder why I was panting so hard. Trust me, you are in no danger of losing your touch," I assured him.

"I am pretty good, aren't I?" he joked.

"The best! But you know who else is good?" I asked. Akio looked off into the distance as if giving my question a lot of thought.

"Tom Daley?" he answered with a mischievous grin. I opened my mouth, closed it and then opened it again.

"Yeah, I'll give you that one, he probably is." Akio chuckled underneath me. "I was talking about me though," I told him.

"Oh really? I don't remember." He shook his head sadly.

"Maybe I should remind you then," I said, already kissing my way down his body.

"I think that would be best." He said the last part as a sigh.

He started out moaning, but after several minutes, he was gripping my hair between his fingers and bucking up into my mouth as he chased his orgasm. My head bobbed up and down between his legs as I took him down my throat. Finally, his body stiffened and he let out a strangled scream as warm streams of cum shot down the back of my throat and coated my tongue. I swallowed it all and then crawled back up his body, licking my lips. Akio's eyes were unfocused when he opened them, but he grabbed me and kissed me fiercely until neither of us could breathe.

"Now do you remember?" I whispered against his lips.

"Uh huh, but I may need a few more reminders here and there. I can be quite forgetful sometimes," Akio whispered back. His lips brushed against mine as they turned up in a smile.

"I'd remind you again this morning if I didn't have to get ready for work, I'm already late though." I kissed him one more time and then rolled out of bed, chuckling at his disappointed whimper. I looked over my shoulder as I walked towards the bathroom and found him staring at my ass. He looked sleepy, sexy, and satisfied and it brought a smile to my face as I started the shower.

A few hours later I was frowning as I stared down at the blueprint and then back up at the man standing in front of me.

"Explain to me once again what happened," I sighed.

"There's no electric run through that wall. The electrician must have missed it in the plans and the drywall was put up before we caught the mistake. It wasn't until I went to charge my phone while I was painting that I realized the problem," Carl explained.

"Okay. Go ahead and get someone to take down the drywall while I call the electrician and ask him to come back. Obviously, we'll have to wait on painting until this has all been fixed," I told him.

"Got it, boss," he said as he walked off.

"Thanks, Carl," I called after him. I shook my head. It was inevitable that something went wrong with each job, but fortunately that one had been a minor problem and Carl had found it in time to make repairs before the inspection. Failing an inspection and having to have it redone was a costly and timely mistake that I wanted to avoid if at all possible.

It had been a month since I saw Matt at the carnival and told him that we were ahead of schedule. He'd been very excited to hear that because, as he told me, he was having to turn kids away. He didn't have the room in their current location to help the rising number of teens who had been coming to the center for help, but the new center would allow him to provide care for all those kids.

I'd never realized the responsibility my job carried until that moment and I refused to let Matt or those kids down. I walked around the building, rolled up blueprints in hand, as I checked over the details of each room myself. I moved into the final room, luckily having found no more problems when my phone rang.

"Hey, baby!" I answered.

"Hi! How's your day going?" Akio asked.

"Okay. We had a little issue with the electrical work, but nothing that's going to set us back too much. How about yours?" I listened as he sighed through the phone.

"I've had better. Last-minute problems with the tour plans, nothing major, just annoying little things that all add up to be a crazy day," he told me.

"I'm sorry, baby. I think we both need a night together where we can leave the stress of our jobs behind," I said, already picturing the two of us curled up on the couch, watching a movie with the lights turned off and a bowl of popcorn in his lap. I'd set the bowl aside and lower him onto his back and when I'd kiss him, his lips would taste like salt and butter. I licked my lips as the image played out clearly in my mind.

"Doesn't that sound perfect?" Akio exclaimed.

"Yes, it really does. I can't wait," I sighed.

"Oh, I'm so glad you think so too. I wasn't sure if you'd want to go, but I promise, we'll have a great time." Hearing the excitement in his voice pulled me back from my daydream. *Wait, what? Where are we going? I thought we were snuggling on the couch.*

"I'll need different clothes than what I have at your house, so why don't you pick me up at my place and we'll go from there, okay?"

"Okay. Tell me again where we're going?" I winced as I asked the question, hoping he wouldn't realize I hadn't been listening.

"Oh yeah, I forgot to tell you which club," Akio said with a laugh. "It's called Lush-Us and it's my favorite. I can't wait to see you out on the dance floor," he purred.

"Me either," I agreed weakly.

I hung up the phone wondering what in the hell I'd just gotten myself into. I'd never been to a club before because they didn't have any—gay or straight—in the small town I'd grown up in. I also had no idea how to dance and I was pretty sure I'd make a fool of myself if I tried. The relaxing night I had envisioned for the two of us had been replaced by a new level of stress. I would go though because it was what Akio wanted to do and I would do anything to make him happy. I just hoped I wouldn't completely embarrass him, and myself, along the way.

I got home and after spending some quality time with Angel, I took a quick shower then stood in front of my open closet, trying to figure out what I was supposed to wear at the trendiest night club in the heart of Chicago. I only knew that much because after I hung up with Akio, I'd quickly googled Lush-Us so I could see what it was like. It was listed as one of the hottest gay clubs in the area and the pictures of the interior showed a huge dance floor on the lower level, a glass walkway above that, which was also used for dancing, and two separate bars on either side of the club.

I looked over my clothing options and groaned in frustration. Somehow, I didn't think my usual jeans and t-shirts were going to work for where we were going. I scrambled to come up with a solution and then I picked up my phone. There was only one person I could think of that would be able to help me right then.

"Hey, man, what's up?" I heard him say.

"Carter, I need your help," I told him, not even caring if he heard the desperation in my voice. After describing the situation and the contents of my closet, he'd laughed and called me hopeless then instructed me to get my ass over to his place.

When I arrived there, Carter and Ryan had circled around me slowly and I'd begun to sweat under their close scrutiny. I'd felt a bit like an animal on the auction block and couldn't help the nervous laugh that escaped when I wondered if they were going to check my ears and teeth next. Finally, they both began speaking at once and it was eerie how in tune they were with each other.

"He's about my size so I'm thinking my black leather pants. They'll show off his ass nicely," Ryan said.

"Definitely. And that tight green shirt you just bought will highlight his eyes," Carter suggested.

"I'll grab my black boots. Oh wait, what size do you wear?" Ryan asked, turning back around and snapping his fingers.

"Twelve?" I answered, although it came out sounding more like a question.

"Perfect," he said.

"Oh! I'll get one of my cuffs and a cord necklace for him to wear," Carter called out, already walking away.

I stood there, not sure what to do as they raced around, gathering the supplies they'd need. Soon, I was dressed and Carter worked some sticky gunk into my hair while Ryan attached the leather cuff to my wrist. When they were finished, they stepped back and let me look at myself in the mirror. The person staring back at me was unfamiliar.

My hair looked like I'd just enjoyed a sheet-clawing round of sex, the shirt looked like it would split apart if I flexed my arms and I just knew that I was going to rip the back of the tight leather pants the moment I sat down. I looked at their excited faces though and didn't have the heart to tell them any of that so I pasted a smile on my face and thanked them instead.

A few minutes later, I was on my way to pick up Akio at his apartment. I hated that he still had some of his belongings there, but we were both waiting until we had a free weekend to make the move complete. I wanted him with me all the time and I'd told him as much. He'd agreed and had already begun to move his things over to my place, but it hadn't happened as quickly as I wanted since we'd both been so busy.

I shifted uncomfortably in my seat, I had no idea how anyone could get used to wearing such tight clothing. However, I comforted myself with the thought that Akio would probably take one look at me, realize how ridiculous I looked and call the whole thing off. Perhaps we could have that quiet movie night after all.

Akio's reaction was not at all what I expected though and I wasn't sure if I should feel disappointed or flattered. I was flattered because his eyes bugged out of his head the minute he saw me and he looked like one of those cartoon characters that was salivating over a big roasted turkey. I was disappointed because judging by his reaction, I wasn't getting out of going to the club that night.

That realization was even harder to accept when I finally noticed what Akio was wearing. I'd been so nervous about his reaction to me that I hadn't taken the time to look him over, but once I had his approval, I let my eyes look their fill and I nearly swallowed my tongue at what I saw.

He was dressed in a tight, black mesh shirt and a pair of red leather pants that curved perfectly around his ass. He wore black boots that laced up and he'd completed the outfit with a thin black collar around his neck which filled my mind with images of Akio tied up and at my mercy while I spanked his ass until it was bright red.

My cock stirred to life and I had to close my eyes and picture gross things like curdled milk, spiders, and my great aunt Millie, who used to pinch my cheeks and give me sloppy, red lipsticky kisses right on the lips, no matter how many times I tried to turn my head. I sighed in relief when I felt my cock settle back down. I could barely breathe in the tight pants Ryan had loaned me, there was definitely no room for a hard-on to happen in there.

"OMG!" Akio exclaimed as he walked around me, checking me out. *Why does everyone keep doing that?* His little joke about my name didn't go unnoticed and I glared at him, but he just laughed.

"No, seriously, you are so fucking hot. I may have to pee on you so everyone knows you're mine and to keep their paws off," he growled.

"Umm…babe, I'm not really into that kind of thing," I teased. "But I can promise you that no one else will ever touch me. I'm all yours. Besides, I think you're the one I need to worry about; look at you."

"Oh! You like this? It was just hanging in the back of my closet," he replied off-handedly.

I pulled him into my arms and kissed him until the room spun and we were both gasping for air. My hands slid down to cup his leather clad butt and I swatted him hard, once. He gasped and I bit his bottom lip, tugging on it gently. He moaned and thrust his hips, rubbing himself against my thigh and I could feel his hard arousal.

"Are you sure you don't want to stay here and take these clothes off instead?" I murmured as I began kissing my way down his neck. He shuddered in my arms, but then pulled back.

"Not on your life! My man is hotter than hell and I can't wait to show him off on the dance floor," he purred. I started to tell him that I couldn't dance, but he grabbed me by the hand, dragging me out of his building and to my truck before I got the chance.

The music was loud as we walked into the club and I could feel the pounding of the bass as it vibrated through my chest. I had no idea what I was doing so I followed Akio as he grabbed my hand and led me over to one of the bars. He shouted our drink orders to the bartender who was built like a tank, with a sleeveless t-shirt that showed off the colorful sleeves of ink down each muscled arm. His eyes slid approvingly over Akio and my back stiffened in response to someone encroaching on my territory. He saw the look in my eyes and winked, probably knowing he could easily bench press me if he wanted to, but he got our drinks and moved on to the next customer instead.

Akio smirked at me as he handed me my drink, having missed nothing. I shrugged my shoulders, not sorry at all about my reaction and turned my back to the bar so I could look around at the rest of the club. It was just as the pictures on the internet had shown, the only differences being the crowd of bodies on the dance floor and the bright lights that seemed to flash in time with the music. More people were lining the glass walkway above; dancing, drinking, or watching the crowd below.

I was happy to see that most of the people there were dressed like me and that my outfit hadn't been some elaborate scheme my cousin and his husband had thought up to make me look like a fool. I still felt completely out of my element though so I was relieved when I saw two familiar faces making their way to us through the crowd.

We took turns hugging Curtis and Jakob and then we made

small talk for a while. I smiled at the way they couldn't seem to keep their hands off each other as they told us what was new with them. It was obvious that they were very much in love and it made me happy that our double date had turned out so well for all four of us. I glanced over at Akio and caught the look in his eyes that told me he'd been thinking the same thing.

After a while, Curtis and Jakob told us goodbye and then they headed back out to dance. I watched their retreating backs, but I could feel Akio's stare. I knew what he was thinking and I wished he would change his mind, but I should've known better. He reached out and took my glass from my hand and set it on the bar behind me then he moved in front of me and slid his body up against mine.

I stared down at him, completely mesmerized by the heat I saw in his eyes. He didn't have to say a word for me to know exactly what he was thinking. I reached up and ran my finger over the collar around his neck and I watched his throat as he swallowed hard. He licked his lips and then leaned up so he could speak into my ear.

"Dance with me," Akio said. The feel of his warm breath sent a shiver down my spine and I gave him a single nod, completely under his spell.

CHAPTER
Seventeen

Akio

HEADS TURNED AS I MADE MY WAY THROUGH THE CROWDED dance floor, Morgan right at my heels and I saw the envy in their eyes that he was with me. *I had news for them all, he was mine and he'd be with me not only that night, but every night after,* I thought proudly. I found an opening and stopped, turning to face him.

A slow song was playing so I wrapped my arms around his neck. His hands automatically went around my waist and he pulled me up against him. I could see the wariness in his eyes, but I didn't understand what had put it there.

"What's wrong?" I said into his ear so he could hear me over the loud music. He turned his head away so I used my fingers on his jaw to get him to face me again. "What?" I mouthed.

"I've never really danced before," he finally admitted, watching me closely for my reaction. My heart tripped over itself at the vulnerability I saw in his eyes and I smiled at him.

"It's okay, just move along with me," I told him, swaying my hips slowly to the music. "Dancing is a lot like sex, just pay attention to your partner's body and move along with him."

Morgan gave me a very heated look and then looked down between us as my hips brushed against his. Finally, he started to move and just as I'd suspected, he was a natural. Maybe it was just because he knew my body so well and could predict my moves, but either way it wasn't long before he was moving his body seductively against mine.

Ariana Grande started singing about walking side to side and I could tell Morgan was feeling more confident, so I stepped back and raised my hands above my head as I turned in a slow circle, rolling my hips. I looked over my shoulder and saw his eyes glaze over as he followed my every move and I hoped he was enjoying the way my ass looked in my leather pants.

By the time I had turned back around, Morgan had all but stopped on the dance floor and was staring at me, his eyes so dark they looked almost black. I let my gaze drop and saw the prominent bulge behind his zipper and my mouth watered. My hands smoothed over his chest and my hips continued to move to the music as I dropped lower and lower in front of him, my hands trailing along the same path until I was nearly on the floor and my hands were covering his groin. I gave a small squeeze and his hips jerked towards me.

I bit my lower lip and gazed at him through lowered lashes as I moved back up his body. He reached for me, but I turned my back to him and bent down, my ass swishing back and forth, tantalizingly over his cock. I had to hold back a laugh when he grabbed my hips and pulled me back against him roughly.

I straightened, my back pressed to his chest, and I felt sweat trickle down my spine as he ran his fingers up the back of my neck. I gasped as his fingers curled underneath the leather collar I was wearing and pulled, not enough to hurt me, I knew Morgan never would, but enough for me to feel the bite of leather as it cut into my skin, threatening my breathing. I'd had my fun teasing him, but he was letting me know, in no uncertain terms, that he was in charge, and God, if that didn't make me want to kneel at his feet right there in front of the entire club. I never knew I had a submissive side, but being with Morgan had allowed many self-discoveries.

"Are you proud of yourself?" he growled in my ear as he thrust his hips forward so that his hardness rubbed right along the crack of my ass. I nodded my head. I knew he wouldn't have been able to hear me even if I could manage to speak at that moment.

"I'll get even," he promised, his breath hot against my ear and I shivered in anticipation.

As soon as the song ended, Morgan grabbed my hand and led me to a tall table in the back corner of the club. He pulled one of the stools out and sat, maneuvering me so that I was standing between his knees. His hand spread over my stomach as he pulled me back against him, the warmth of his palm burning my skin through the mesh of my shirt.

A waiter wearing tight pants and no shirt came and took our drink order. He winked at Morgan and I growled low in my chest. Morgan must have felt the vibrations against his chest because he chuckled in my ear and I turned my chin so I could see him.

"Glad to know I'm not the only one who gets jealous." He was wearing the smirk I loved so much and I suddenly wished we were alone so I could do dirty things to him.

The waiter came back with our drinks and I sipped mine as I looked around. From our vantage point, we could see everything going on in front as well as above us. My eyes scanned the room, watching the sweaty, writhing dancers as they ground their hips against each other. Some were dancing so erotically that it looked like they were actually having sex on the dance floor.

"Look up there," Morgan whispered in my ear. I moved my focus to the glass floor above us and scanned the walkway, searching for what had caught Morgan's attention. I gave him a questioning look over my shoulder when I didn't see anything out of the ordinary.

"The twink and the bear," he said.

My eyes swept over the crowd above until I found the couple he'd described. One of the men, the bear, appeared to be in his early forties while the other one, the twink, looked like he was barely twenty-one. The older man was wearing leather pants and a matching leather vest with no shirt. His big, muscular arms glistened with sweat as he wrapped one arm securely behind the younger man. At first, I didn't notice anything other than the fact that they were locked in a heated kiss, but then my eyes traveled lower and I sucked in a breath. *How had I missed that before?*

"You see it now?" Morgan said, his hot breath fanning across my neck. I nodded, unable to turn away from the sight before me. "Keep watching them," he ordered.

I felt Morgan's fingers coasting over the waistband of my pants as I stared transfixed at the couple. The older man continued to kiss the younger man passionately, but what I'd missed the first time was the way his hand was moving between their two bodies. The muscles in his arm rippled and bunched as he stroked their two cocks together between his meaty fist.

"Look at the expression on the younger man's face," Morgan whispered as he ran one finger through the sweat on my spine and then let it dip below my waistband.

The look on the twink's face was nothing short of ecstasy. His eyes rolled up in his head as the larger man continued to work them both over, not giving him a second's pause. Goose bumps broke out over my skin despite the fever I was certain was burning just below the surface.

Morgan undid the snap of my pants to loosen them and then stuck his hand further inside the back. His finger, slick from my sweat, slid between my ass cheeks and began circling my hole. I let my head drop back to his shoulder as he pressed just the tip of one inside me. My eyes fluttered shut at the feel of him stretching me, but they popped back open at the sound of his stern command.

"Keep your eyes on them. If you let them shut, I'll stop," he threatened. I forced my eyes to remain open. The things he was doing to me, the way he played my body like a fine-tuned instrument was too good to let it stop. I needed his hands on me, in me, touching me everywhere all at once, more than I needed to breathe.

The older man had moved his free hand up and was gripping the other man by the hair. The younger man appeared to be saying something, a look of clear desperation on his face and I knew that he was begging the man to let him come. The older man shook his head no, but refused to slow the movement of his hand.

Morgan continued to thrust his finger in and out of me, going a little deeper each time and adding an occasional twist to his wrist. My vision clouded and my legs felt wobbly as my weeping cock pushed painfully against my zipper, begging to be let free. I thrust my hips, looking for any kind of friction, but whimpered in frustration when I found none.

"Please," I begged even though I knew Morgan couldn't hear me and I watched as the younger man repeated the same word.

"Almost there," Morgan whispered huskily and I wasn't sure if he meant me or the twink above us, perhaps both.

I was right on the edge, but I needed a final push, something to send me soaring. The older man stared into the younger man's eyes and nodded his head as his hand began to move faster. The younger man opened his mouth and the older man's mouth slammed down over his, silencing what I'm sure would've been a loud scream.

Morgan used his other hand to turn my head and his tongue swept into my mouth at the same moment that he moved his finger, letting it graze over that perfect spot. Sparks flew past my eyes and I choked on a scream of my own as my orgasm raced through me, my cock erupting inside my pants.

He swallowed my cries and then pulled his hand out of my pants and turned me to face him. I was shaking as I wrapped my arms around his neck and buried my face in his chest. Morgan gathered me in close and whispered soft words in my ear as his hands smoothed up and down my back.

When I had quit trembling, I looked up and my eyes met his. The complete love and devotion I saw there, brought tears to my eyes and I had to fight to swallow past the lump in my throat. Morgan leaned forward and kissed the wetness from my eyelids and then wiped it away with his thumbs.

"I love you," he breathed against my lips and I kissed him in response and then leaned back so I could see his gorgeous sea-green eyes.

"Will you take me home?" I asked. He smiled sweetly as he nodded his head.

I told him I'd be right back and excused myself to go to the bathroom. The music seemed too loud in my ears and the lights too bright after such an intimate moment and I immediately missed the bubble Morgan and I had created for ourselves.

I wove through the crowd and opened the door to the restroom, thankful when I found it empty. I wet a few paper towels and disappeared into a stall to clean myself up as much as possible for the car ride home. When I was finished, I opened the door and stepped out, but stopped in surprise when I came face to face with Garrett. He was standing near the sinks with his arms crossed as if he'd been waiting for me.

"What are you doing here?" I asked, pasting a smile on my face even though I could tell something wasn't right.

"I was waiting for you, I wanted to talk," he replied. I moved past him and began washing my hands at the sink. I looked at him in the mirror.

"Okay, I have just a minute, but then I need to get back out there. Morgan's waiting on me, we were just getting ready to leave," I explained.

"This will only take a minute," he said. I turned to face him, giving him my undivided attention. He uncrossed his arms, but he seemed nervous as he tilted his head to look at me.

"Garrett, we've been friends a long time. It seems like something's been bothering you for a while now. You've always been able to talk to me about anything so just tell me what's going on," I said. He let out a puff of air.

"I don't like seeing you with that guy," he told me. My eyes widened in surprise. That was not what I was expecting him to say at all.

"That guy? You mean Morgan?" I asked, sure that I was hearing him wrong.

"Yes, Morgan," he stated clearly.

"And why is that?" I asked cautiously.

"Because you can do so much better," he said as he began slowly moving closer to me.

"Better. And who exactly would be better for me than Morgan?" I could feel myself starting to get angry, but I wanted to remain as calm as possible. Garrett was one of my closest friends after all.

"Me," he whispered.

I was stunned by his words, but even more so when he grabbed my shoulders and pulled me against him, his mouth crashing down over mine, our teeth clanking together as he took me in a bruising kiss. My eyes widened and it took me just a second before my thought processes caught up and I was able to push him away.

As he fell back, my gaze caught movement over his shoulder and I found myself staring into a set of green eyes. I registered shock and hurt and anger in those green orbs and I felt my heart shatter, but then he moved his sights onto Garrett and the next thing I knew Garrett was on the floor, his hands in the air to ward off another attack as Morgan stood over him. It had all happened so quickly that I hadn't even seen him throw the punch.

I heard someone shouting outside the door and then it slammed open just as Morgan lifted Garrett up by the shirt collar and pulled his arm back, ready to deliver another blow. Jakob grabbed Morgan by the arm and pulled him back against his chest, holding onto him so he couldn't lunge for Garrett.

"I don't want to ban you from the club, Morgan. You're my friend so please, don't make me do that. Just go outside and cool off for a little bit, okay?" Jakob begged him.

Morgan's chest heaved with exertion and his face was twisted in anger. I wanted to go to him, to somehow explain and reassure him that I loved him and only him, but his body language screamed "back off!" He yanked himself out of Jakob's grasp and with one final look my way, stormed out of the bathroom.

I started to follow him, but stopped when I heard Garrett call my name. I turned and looked down at him. He was sitting on the floor, cradling his nose in his hands as blood dripped between his fingers. His eyes pleaded with me to stay and as angry as I was at the mess he'd created, a part of me was still able to recognize my friend.

"We'll talk, I promise, but right now Morgan's hurting more than you are and I'm the only one who can fix this. I need to find him," I told him.

I saw the sadness and the resignation in his eyes and it felt like a blade going through me, but I pushed it aside because the most important thing, the *only* thing that mattered right then was finding Morgan. I knew exactly what that must have looked like to him, what it would've reminded him of, but he needed to know that I wasn't like David, I would never betray him. Curtis was standing just outside the bathroom, looking concerned.

"Where did Morgan go?" I asked frantically.

"He headed towards the front door. Are you okay?" Curtis asked. I didn't bother to answer, not that I could. I was confused by everything that had just happened, but I didn't have time to process any of it. I had to get to Morgan.

I moved quickly through the crowded club, shoving anyone who dared to get in my way and ignoring their shouts of outrage. Finally, I reached the front door and I swung it open, racing outside into the cool night air. My heart pounded painfully in my chest and my head swiveled back and forth as my eyes searched the dark parking lot for one man.

I wanted to sob with relief when I saw his truck, exactly where we'd left it and him standing beside it, staring straight at me. I made myself walk instead of running like I wanted to when I saw the mask that was firmly in place, hiding his emotions from me.

I wasn't sure what his reaction to me would be. Would he yell at me? Curse me? Would he tell me to walk away and never come near him again? I knew I hadn't done anything wrong, but given Morgan's history, would he give me the chance to explain or would my fairy-tale romance end even though it seemed like it had just begun?

I could see his body vibrating as he watched me approach. I moved cautiously, my body also trembling the closer I got, but as angry as he was, I never worried that Morgan would hurt me; I knew he didn't have it in him.

"You stayed," I said quietly. He nodded once and I could see his jaw clenching in the light of the streetlamp. "Can we talk?" I asked.

It seemed like an eternity before he moved. He walked towards me and my breath caught in my throat, but then he brushed past me and my heart plummeted until I heard a sound and I turned and saw him standing beside the open passenger door. Tears streamed down my face, but I couldn't speak over the well of emotion clogging my throat so I simply walked towards him and climbed into his truck. The symbolism behind his gesture spoke volumes and gave me hope.

CHAPTER
Eighteen

Morgan

THE DRIVE HOME WAS A BLUR AS THE SCENE I'D WALKED IN ON replayed in my mind, over and over again on a painfully endless loop. I'd decided to check on Akio when he seemed to be taking longer than expected in the bathroom. Fighting my way through the mass of bodies, I'd finally made my way down the corridor that led to the restrooms and a janitor's closet.

I'd opened the door and it took my brain a few seconds to piece together what I was seeing. Akio was in there, but he wasn't alone. In fact, he was kissing another man and for just a second, I pictured him standing in the shower, the other man's arms wrapped around him as they kissed passionately. I forced the image from my mind. It was Akio in front of me, not David, I reminded myself. But with that reminder came a whole new wave of emotions, the first being rage.

When I'd caught David cheating, I felt hurt because I'd been betrayed by two people who I thought I could trust. I'd felt like a fool as I'd wondered if they'd laughed at how they were pulling one over on me and then I'd felt disgusted that I had ever been their friend when they didn't know the meaning of the word.

With Akio, my reaction was completely different. I remembered Landon telling me that if the same thing happened with the *right* man then it would feel as if my heart had been put through a shredder and that was exactly what it felt like when I saw Akio with another man. My heart refused to believe what my eyes had seen though, so I forced myself to take a moment and really look at what was happening. It was only then that I was able to clearly see the man I loved, the man I trusted with my life and I realized that he wasn't kissing the man back, in fact, he was pushing him away. Relief flooded my veins.

That relief soon turned into a red haze as it sank in that some other man had dared to touch what was mine. My eyes met Akio's and the look on his face told me that he was witnessing the myriad of emotions playing out inside of me, but I couldn't say anything to him because I was too caught up in an anger like I'd never felt before. I felt like I was watching someone else, like I was outside of my body as I grabbed the man when he fell towards me, jerking him around at the same time I pulled my arm back.

It wasn't until my fist connected with his nose, a sharp cracking noise rang through my ears, that I recognized the man. It wasn't some random guy who had seen my boyfriend on the dance floor, thought he was hot and decided to make a move. No, this was personal, someone who Akio was close to. Did I get it all wrong? Was there something more between Akio and Garrett than just friendship? Had I once again been played a fool?

Anger rushed through me once again and I pulled my arm back for another swing at him, but I was suddenly yanked away from Garrett and pressed against a very large, hard chest. I heard Jakob's voice telling me to go outside and calm down and his voice helped to clear some of the haze away.

I looked into Akio's brown eyes, the ones that I had stared into just moments before, feeling like I could see into the depths of his soul and I felt the floor beginning to vibrate under my feet. I turned and walked out, making my way through the crowd and idly wondering if anyone else felt the earth moving around them.

I pushed through the door and gulped in a huge lungful of fresh air, hoping it would help clear my head, but I choked on it instead and I bent over with my hands on my knees. My stomach churned and the ground shook. My teeth began to chatter and it finally occurred to me that it wasn't the earth that was moving, it was me. My heart raced and sweat ran down the sides of my face like I'd just finished running a marathon and my body was shaking so hard that my muscles ached with the strain of holding myself together.

When the shaking subsided to mild tremors and my stomach had settled enough that I knew I wasn't going to throw up, I stood and made my way towards my truck. The only thought in my head was getting as far away from that club and what had happened as possible. I wanted to go home and hide under my covers and forget that the rest of the world existed, if even for a little while.

A nagging voice inside my head kept telling me to stop, to wait, to turn around and not walk away from the best thing that had ever happened to me. My feet slowed as I continued on my path, but the voice wouldn't let up. It warned me that if I walked away, that I'd be making a huge mistake; one that I might regret for the rest of my life. I reached the tailgate of my truck and grabbed onto the edge of it as that voice screamed at me, begging and pleading for me to listen.

I drew in a deep breath and forced myself to turn around and that's when I saw it. The door to the club crashed open and Akio came barreling through it, his head moving from side to side as he frantically searched for something. I continued to stare at him and I knew the moment he found what he was looking for because his eyes connected with mine and his body sagged as if in relief.

Our eyes remained locked as he slowly moved towards me and I could see the wariness in his eyes the closer he got. Shame washed over me. Was Akio frightened of me? Did he think that I could ever possibly hurt him? Finally, he was only a few feet away and he stopped, his voice barely more than a whisper when he spoke.

"You stayed," he said and the surprise in his voice cut me. My jaw clenched and I wasn't sure what to say just yet because my emotions were still in the process of changing every few seconds so I nodded instead.

"Can we talk?" he asked gently. I stared at him for just a moment and then I walked around him and opened his door.

Because of course, I would.

Because I had made a promise to him that I would never make him feel unimportant ever again and even though my heart felt bruised and battered, it was still important to me to keep that promise.

We stepped inside the cabin and I dropped my keys on the table then went to the kitchen. I heard Akio's footsteps as he followed me, but I busied myself with grabbing a bag and filling it with ice. I wrapped a towel around it and then sank down into one of the chairs and laid my hand out on the table, inspecting it. Akio moved closer and I heard him gasp when he saw the bruises forming on my knuckles. I flexed my hand, taking inventory and finding no significant damage.

"It'll be fine, it's not broken," I tried to tell him, but my voice cracked on the last word and I felt my eyes filling with tears. I had never felt a pain like the one I felt at the thought of losing him, losing what we'd worked so hard to build together. I stared down at my hand as I tried to rein in my emotions. *Akio's not David. This isn't the same thing*, the voice told me.

He sat down in the chair next to me and reached for my hand, gently cradling it in his own. I held my breath as he bent his head and carefully pressed his lips to my knuckles then he covered my hand with the ice and held it there. My eyes found his and we sat there, neither of us speaking a word, but still saying so much.

I saw it then, all the worry and the anguish, the compassion and caring. I saw the love and the trust, but most of all I saw the truth. I looked into those deep brown eyes and I saw the heart and soul of Akio Forrest and I knew, I knew that he would never betray me, not even for a second. All I'd needed to do was to step outside of my own head, my own doubts, and I would've seen that the truth was right there, literally staring me in the face.

He smiled at me as he saw the understanding in my eyes and I reached for him, ignoring the pain in my hand as I cupped his face. He leaned in, meeting me in the middle and our mouths found each other in the sweetest of kisses. The kiss soon turned heated and I became filled with the overwhelming need to stake my claim on him, to remind him of who he belonged to. The feeling swept through me with such ferocity that it stole my breath. It was urgent and it was primal and there was no fighting it.

We stood at the same time, our chairs scraping across the floor and the ice landing at our feet as that familiar electricity sparked to life between us. We frantically began tearing at each other's clothes, each of us desperate to have nothing between us. When all our clothing lay in a heap on the floor, I lifted him in my arms and carried him to the bedroom.

I laid him down and then grabbed the supplies from the drawer next to the bed and tossed them beside him. He watched me as I crawled onto the bed and covered his body with my own. I stared into those warm chocolate eyes of his and I saw everything I'd ever wanted within their depths.

"Who do you belong to?" I asked, emotions making my voice sound gruff.

"I'm yours, Morgan. I've been yours since the day I met you," he said without any hesitation.

I stared at him for several seconds, my chest brushing against his as I breathed and then I moved off him and rolled onto my back. Akio sat up, staring down at me in confusion. I picked up the condom and handed it to him.

"Show me that you're mine," I told him.

Flames burned in his eyes as he snatched the condom from my hand and crawled down the bed. I lifted my head to watch as he grabbed the bottle of lube and poured some onto his fingers. He wrapped his lips around the head of my dick at the same time his arm reached around behind him. I could tell the moment his fingers found their mark because he groaned low in his throat, the vibrations sending delicious sensations down the length of me.

My cock grew harder, almost to the point of being painful as I watched him rocking back and forth, pleasuring himself while also pleasuring me. When I couldn't take it one more second, I reached under his arms and dragged him up my body.

"I need to be inside you. I need to feel a part of you that no one else will ever touch," I whispered, not caring how vulnerable it made me sound.

Akio's expression was serious and his eyes never left mine as he slid the condom down my cock and slicked it with lube. His legs straddled my sides as he lowered himself onto me. I saw him struggle to relax enough to take me all the way, but still his eyes remained locked on mine. He eased down slowly until his ass rested on my lap. He sighed and it was the sound of home and love and *finally*. He reached for my hands and I held them out to him, threading my fingers with his.

"Every single part of me, everything I have to give, is yours and no one else's," he promised.

"I know. I knew all along, I just needed to be reminded," I told him.

"Good," he said and my eyes rolled up inside my head as he began to rock his hips back and forth. He continued that for several minutes, each of us relishing the feeling of our bodies being joined together. Suddenly he stopped and my eyes sprung open, only to find his face inches away from mine.

"Who do you belong to, Morgan Greene?" he asked, throwing my words back at me.

"You, always you," I swore. A devilish smirk formed on his lips and he leaned down so his mouth was next to my ear.

"Show me," Akio whispered.

My body suddenly felt like it was on fire and I quickly pulled him off of me and flipped him over so that he was on his stomach, ass in the air. My hand came down hard across his backside and he moaned as his body jerked.

"Yes, please, Morgan, more," he cried.

I lined my cock up at his entrance and my hand flew through the air, connecting with his flesh at the same time I slammed into him. Akio screamed his pleasure and his hands clawed at the sheets as he tried to find something to anchor him. I grabbed his wrists and pulled them behind his back, clasping them in one of my hands as I continued to thrust in and out of him.

He continued begging me for more until his words turned into incoherent little whimpers and I felt my balls drawing up tight against my body. I adjusted my angle, guaranteeing that I'd hit his prostate with every forward thrust and he screamed at the exact moment I felt him tighten around me, squeezing my cock in a viselike grip.

I shouted his name as my orgasm hit and I spilled over into the condom, wishing for a day when even that wouldn't come between us. I knew it would though, with a surety that I'd never felt before. It was as if through that experience, we'd found a way to connect with each other on an even deeper level and the burdens of the past no longer carried the same weight.

I cleaned us both up and then curled around Akio and held him as we both drifted off to sleep. I knew that no matter what else came our way, we would face it together. We'd weathered a storm of monstrous proportions that night and we'd come out the victors.

Akio fought a laugh as he helped straighten my tie, but the twitching of his lips gave him away. My hands were on his hips and every time I dipped my head forward to get a kiss, he'd pull back, just out of my reach, teasing me. I tried again and growled as he darted out of the way.

He yelped as I yanked him towards me, sliding a hand around the back of his neck and pressed our lips together. Our tongues swirled around each other and I felt him melt into me. After a few minutes, I released him, pleased at the dazed look in his eyes. He shook his head as if to clear it and then finished fixing my tie.

"There, all done. Tell me what you think," he said, admiring his handiwork. I stood up from where I'd been leaning against the bathroom sink and turned to look in the mirror.

"It's perfect," I replied, looking at his reflection instead of my own. He blushed when he caught my stare. He was dressed in a black suit with a pale purple shirt and a tie that was a deeper shade of purple. I thought he looked stunning, but I still would've rather seen him *out* of the suit.

I checked my hair quickly, and ran my hands down the front of my tie. I was also dressed in a black suit, but I was wearing the blue shirt and darker blue tie that Akio had picked out for me. He'd been excited to choose my outfit for the day, saying that we needed to look our very best because it wasn't every day that we got to go to a wedding at a mega-mansion. I wasn't sure what the big deal was since Lachlan and Rylie had only invited their closest friends and they'd managed to keep the paparazzi from finding out so there was little chance of getting our picture taken, but it was a big deal to Akio so I went along with it and let him dress me.

It had been a month since the incident at the club and Akio still hadn't spoken to Garrett, not that he hadn't tried. At first, I'd baulked at the idea of Garrett being anywhere near him, but then I noticed how sad Akio looked whenever he mentioned his friend and I realized that I was being selfish. I told Akio that his happiness meant more to me than anything else and if keeping Garrett as a friend was that important to him, then I would understand and support him.

Akio had shown his appreciation many times that night and the next day he'd begun calling Garrett. He'd left dozens of voicemails and text messages, but he hadn't responded. I hugged Akio and told him to be patient, that Garrett probably just needed some time, but a part of me wondered. All I knew was that I hated seeing Akio so upset.

Garrett was the only dark blemish on our otherwise happy life together. Akio and I had moved the rest of his things into the cabin the day after the club fiasco and he'd let his landlord know that he was giving up his lease. I'd asked him if he was alright with moving outside of the city and he assured me that he already thought of the cabin as home and that he'd gotten used to the quiet at night. Then he'd informed me, in a very sassy tone, that I would just have to agree to be his errand boy if he got a craving for sushi in the middle of the night since there were no sushi restaurants that would deliver that far out. I'd agreed and then proceeded to spank the sass right out of him.

The Agape House project was nearly complete with only a few finishing touches needed before I could schedule the final inspection. Everyone had been busily preparing for the grand opening, set for two weeks from then.

I held Akio's hand as we left the house and on the way to the wedding. I blew out a puff of air as I pulled past the iron gate and got my first look at Lachlan and Rylie's home. The place looked like it belonged on the cover of Forbes magazine and I finally understood why Akio had been so excited to go there.

The wedding was held in the backyard where white silk had been draped throughout the trees, creating an elaborate canopy overhead. It was small and intimate and perfect for the couple who didn't seem to like having attention drawn to themselves. When the preacher asked who was giving the grooms away, Kerry and Benjamin, the older couple who I'd been told were like parents to Lachlan growing up and then to Rylie as well, stood together and presented the two men to each other.

Micah stood beside Lachlan and Rylie's bandmate, Steve, stood beside him as the grooms exchanged their vows. I squeezed Akio's hand as we listened to them promise to be each other's strength in times of weakness and to fill their home with love and joy and children. Everyone laughed when Rylie amended that maybe not *every* room needed to be filled with children, considering the size of their home.

There wasn't a dry eye in the house though as Micah said a few words in memory of Lachlan's brother, Spencer, who had died while serving in the military, followed by Lachlan and Rylie lighting a candle in his honor.

The reception was held near the massive swimming pool with tables and chairs set up along its edges and beautiful white candles floating on top of the water. Caterers served a delicious dinner and a live band provided quiet background music. We stayed until late into the evening, everyone content just to talk and spend time together, until I noticed Akio yawning into his hand and then we excused ourselves and headed home.

I lay in the dark, long after he'd fallen asleep on my chest, running my fingers through his hair and thinking over the perfect evening we'd had. Listening to Lachlan and Rylie recite their vows and seeing the love and happiness between them had started a yearning inside of me, a longing for something…more. Akio mumbled something in his sleep and then burrowed his face into my neck and in the wee hours of the night, with the sound of Akio breathing evenly in my ear, an idea began to take shape.

CHAPTER
Nineteen

Akio

I HUNG UP MY PHONE AND SIGHED BEFORE STARTING MY CAR AND pulling away from the curb. I'd been running errands all morning and decided to try calling Garrett again, just as I had every day for the last month and a half, but like each of my previous attempts, it went straight to his voicemail.

I hadn't told Travis or Jasper what had happened, figuring that it should be Garrett's decision to tell them if he wanted them to know, but I had asked if they'd heard from him. Garrett had told them that he was very busy working towards a deadline and couldn't be disturbed. They'd bought his story because they didn't have any reason not to, but I knew better; I knew he was avoiding me and it hurt.

My mind raced with questions like had I done or said something to lead him on or that would make him think I felt the same way.

When had his feelings for me started and why? Could our friendship survive what had happened? I'd turned those questions and more over in my head until I had begun to make myself crazy. There was only one person who had the answers, but he was refusing to speak to me. My phone rang just as I was finishing up at the bank and I fished it out of my pocket as I unlocked my car and climbed inside.

"Hey, sexy!" I said.

"Hey, baby! I missed waking up with you this morning." My heart skipped a beat at the sound of Morgan's deep voice through the phone.

"Believe me, getting out of a bed that I'd been sharing with my warm and snuggly man was the last thing I wanted to do, but I had a million errands to run before the grand opening later," I explained.

"Well, it just so happens that I had some errands of my own to run. I'm in the city if you have time to meet me for a cup of coffee," he said and I smiled for the first time that day. Any time I got to spend with Morgan sounded perfect to me. He wasn't far from where I was so I told him to sit tight and I'd be there soon.

I parked along the curb near the coffee shop and made sure I had my phone before locking my car and walking up the sidewalk. I pulled the heavy door open and breathed in the delicious aroma of freshly ground coffee. It wasn't too busy at that time of day and my eyes scanned the few patrons for Morgan. My eyes widened though when they landed on Garrett instead.

He was sitting at a small table at the back of the shop and he quickly stood when he saw me. He started walking towards me and I swallowed hard, my head turning from one side to the other in search of Morgan. I knew he was fine with me talking to Garrett, but I didn't want there to be any misunderstandings if he were to walk in and find me with the man who had kissed me.

"Don't worry, Morgan's okay with us being here. In fact, he's the one who set this whole thing up," Garrett explained.

"He did?" I asked, shocked. Garrett motioned for me to sit down and so I joined him at the table. A waitress came over and took our order and then left. He had dark circles under his eyes like he hadn't slept in days, or even longer and he looked thinner than usual.

"Yeah, Morgan started pounding on my door early this morning and basically told me that I needed to get my head out of my ass and talk things out with you before I lost you for good. Then he said some other things, but I'm not going to repeat them. Suffice it to say, your boyfriend can be a scary man when he wants to be and he has some pretty strange ideas about where he can shove his foot." I chuckled and Garrett smiled although it didn't reach his eyes.

"I've been trying to get ahold of you," I said.

"I wasn't ready to talk yet. I'm still not, but I owe you some answers," he said quietly.

The waitress came back with our coffees and placed them in front of us on the table. I picked mine up and held it in my hands to give them something to do. Garrett paid closer attention than necessary to the stir stick in his cup.

"Did I cause all of this? Was it something I did wrong?" The questions that had been plaguing me ever since that night came out before I could stop them. Garrett looked up in surprise and his eyes softened when he saw my distress.

"Yes and no, Akio," he answered and I felt even more confused than before. "Yes, it's because of you, but no, you didn't do anything wrong. My feelings for you started simply because of who you are; an amazing, kind, funny, and gorgeous man," he whispered. We stared at each other for a few seconds and then we both dropped our gazes to the table.

"When?" I breathed. I didn't have to say anymore because I knew Garrett would understand.

"I'm not sure when exactly. You and I have always been close. For some reason, I've found it easier to talk to you than just about anyone else in the world and I guess somewhere along the way, the connection I'd always felt with you turned into more." He shrugged his shoulders. I remained quiet, letting him tell me in his own way and time.

"I kept waiting for the right time to say something, but I was afraid of ruining things between us," he admitted with a humorless laugh. "Then Morgan came into the picture and I could see how much you liked him and it scared me. It scared me because I could feel you slipping further and further away. When I saw you at the club that night and saw how close you and Morgan had gotten, I knew that if I didn't take a chance and tell you how I felt that I'd regret it forever. Turns out, I do anyway," he murmured.

My heart ached as I watched my friend struggling. I wanted to go to him and hug him and that's exactly what I would have done in the past, but because of what had happened that night at the club, there was a wall between us, a line that couldn't be crossed. I hated it, but I respected it too.

"You know I care about you, right? You're my friend and I love you," I said, looking at him so he'd see how much I meant it. He looked back at me and I saw sadness in his eyes.

"Just not the way I want you to, right?" His gaze held with mine as if challenging me to deny it.

"No," I whispered. He nodded his head, his lips pressed into a thin line.

"I need to get going," he said suddenly and I grabbed his wrist without thinking, afraid that would be the last time I'd see him.

"Where are you going?" He looked down at where my hand held his wrist and I let go, sliding my hand back.

"I'm not sure. I need some time away from everybody and everything," he told me.

"Will you be back?" I asked and my voice sounded scratchy around the tears I was holding in.

"Do you want me to?" His head tilted as he studied my reaction.

"Of course, I do. You're my friend, you idiot," I blurted without thinking. Garrett laughed and that time it sounded genuine.

"Then I'll be back. Eventually," he agreed. I watched him as he got up to leave, but then he stopped and stared down at me. He seemed to be weighing his next words carefully.

"I'm really sorry if I caused any problems between you and Morgan," he said.

"We'll be alright," I assured him and he sighed.

"Good. You're a great guy, Akio, and you deserve to be happy." Garrett bent down and kissed my forehead, just a gentle sweep of his lips and then he was gone.

I sat there for a while. My heart felt heavy, yet a little lighter after talking to him. I hoped that Garrett would be okay and that we'd be able to reestablish our friendship at some point, but only time would tell. I took a sip of my coffee and grimaced when I found that it had turned cold. I stood up and walked towards the door, the sunlight hitting my face as I stepped out onto the sidewalk. I took a deep breath, a small smile beginning at the edges of my mouth. Garrett had told me to be happy and I knew just where to start.

I stood in the shower and let the warm water beat down on me, easing the tension in my muscles. I'd come home and taken one look at Morgan's loving face and I'd fallen apart, the emotions of the day overwhelming me. He let me cry on him until there were no more tears and then he listened as I told him everything that had happened between me and Garrett.

I could see the worry in Morgan's eyes that he'd done the wrong thing by getting Garrett to meet me at the coffee shop so I'd rushed to assure him. If he hadn't gotten Garrett to talk to me, he may have taken off without a word and I may not have ever heard from him again. As painful as it had been to see my friend in pain, at least I'd had the chance to try and smooth things over and to let him know I cared and with any luck, Garrett would come back someday.

I tilted my head and sighed as Morgan's lips pressed against the side of my neck. He reached around me and poured soap into his palm then began lathering my skin, washing my stress away. I leaned my head back on his shoulder and closed my eyes, just letting the feel of his hands on my skin soothe the jagged edges of my soul and put me back together. His hands moved lower and I gasped as he wrapped his soapy hand around my cock. My hips punched forward of their own accord and I slid through his tight grip and then back again.

His palm splayed across my stomach and then moved up to tweak my nipple as his fist continued to stroke me. I moaned loudly and the sound echoed around the walls of the shower. Morgan's hand moved faster and his grip tightened around my shaft and then loosened with a twist of his wrist every time he reached the head.

I reached up and locked my wrists together around his neck, clinging to him as he carried me away to a place where nothing existed except for the feel of his hands on my body. Morgan moved his hand faster as my breathing became erratic and my heart threatened to leap out of my chest.

"Morgan," I shouted and then I was flying. My legs felt weak, but I didn't need to worry about falling because he lifted me up into his arms. My legs wrapped around his waist and he carried me into our bedroom where he set me down and then began drying me off with a towel. I tried to reach for him, wanting to make him feel good too, but he shook his head.

"This was about you," he told me.

I looked up at him and wondered what it was I'd ever done to deserve a man like Morgan Greene and then I smiled when I realized that he was looking back at me the same way. I supposed we both were lucky to have found each other and in this crazy, messed-up world, if you were lucky enough to find that someone special, then you better hold on tight and not let go. At least, that was the plan with Morgan and me because he was my happy place, my true north, my soulmate.

A couple of hours later we walked around the building of the new Agape House. Morgan led the group, the people who had originally developed the plan to expand and renew the LGBTQA teen center and I saw how impressed they were as they saw what all our hard work had brought forth. My heart filled with pride as I listened to Morgan tell them that the center would now be able to serve hundreds more teens each day than it was currently able to do. Matt's eyes lit up when he heard that and he and Isaac shared an excited look.

"You've done a brilliant job. I'd like to talk to you later about another project I'm interested in starting," Lachlan told Morgan, but Rylie stopped him before he could go any further.

"No shop talk. You can talk business any other night you want, but tonight is for celebrating," he scolded his husband gently.

"You're right, I'm sorry." Lachlan kissed Rylie on the lips and then slipped Morgan his business card when his husband wasn't looking. "Call me tomorrow," he whispered.

Morgan smiled and slipped the card into his pocket before turning towards the rest of the group which was comprised of friends and family. His parents had come to Chicago to partake in the grand opening celebration and had immediately hit it off with my parents who were there as well. Our mothers, in particular, became fast friends and I'd caught them over in the corner whispering to each other on more than one occasion. The first time I'd caught them, I'd looked to Morgan for help, but he'd just shrugged his shoulders and said that it beat the alternative. I had to agree, but it was still a little unsettling.

"You did an amazing job," Caleb said, giving Morgan a hug. Carter was next, saying that he never had a doubt. Morgan thanked them, but modestly protested that it was very much a group effort.

"It was a group effort," Landon agreed. "But because a lot of our group was busy with other projects, the bulk of the responsibility landed on the shoulders of you two." He pointed to Morgan and me. "You two make a pretty great team if I do say so myself."

Everyone cheered that sentiment and I felt my face flush with embarrassment and maybe just a hint of pride. I glanced at my watch and saw that it was nearly time for the rest of the guests to arrive so I started to suggest that we move back down to the main entrance when Morgan began speaking. I turned to face him and froze when I saw him with one knee on the floor in front of me. My eyes shot up to the rest of the group, hoping they could explain what was happening, but the excited looks on their faces told me that they were in on the surprise. My mother's eyes were glossy and a huge smile lit her face as she held onto my dad and then I looked back down at Morgan who was waiting patiently for my full attention.

"I never expected to find someone like you when I moved to Chicago, in fact, I wasn't even looking, but I suppose it's right what they say about finding love when you least expect it because you turned out to be the best surprise and my greatest joy. You've taught me how to laugh at the simplest things, how to trust someone else with my heart, and how to love more fiercely than I ever thought possible. I came here thinking I was broken, but you showed me that that was not the case; all I needed was the right partner and once we found each other, we became stronger together."

Tears ran down my face as I watched him pull a small black box from his pocket and open it up. Inside, were two matching silver bands. He lifted the smaller of the two out of the box and held it up as he took my hand in his.

"Akio Forrest, I love you with all my heart and I want to spend the rest of my life proving it to you. Will you marry me?"

"Yes," I said through my tears, nodding my head for emphasis.

I watched as he slid the ring onto my finger and then I was wrapping my arms around his neck and kissing him as he stood up to his full height, lifting my feet off the floor. Everyone cheered around us and there were a few tears other than my own, but it was okay because they were all happy tears. Once he set me back on the floor, they all took turns congratulating us. Ryan whispered something to his husband who then shouted a loud "Yes!" while pumping his fist in the air.

"I guess Cryan won't be the only bad name around anymore," he said excitedly. We all looked at him in confusion so he went on to explain. "When you two get married, you'll be Forrest-Greene," he said with a laugh.

I turned to Morgan and his eyes were as wide as mine. *How had we never realized that before?* Then he grabbed me and kissed me until I forgot about silly names and grand openings and even the fact that our mothers were standing where they could see us. The only thought going through my mind at that moment was that as happy as I was right then, I knew that it was just the beginning of the happiness I would experience in my future with Morgan.

EPILOGUE

Isaac

I smiled as I looked around at the new building. The new center was much bigger than the old facility and we'd be able to help so many more kids. Lately, we'd seen a rise in teens that had been kicked out of their homes or needed to run away to escape an abusive parent or were just living in such terrible conditions that they needed a helping hand. Whatever their reason for coming to the center, they all had one thing in common, they were all members of the LGBTQA community.

It hadn't been that long ago that I was one of the teenagers that needed the center. I didn't allow myself to think about the circumstances that had led me to seek refuge at Agape House very often, choosing to focus on the positive things that had happened since I first walked through those doors instead.

Agape House had changed the course of my life, just as it had done and would continue to do for countless other teens and it was all because of the man standing next to me. Matt was the first face I saw when I walked through those doors so many years ago. I'd been wary of him at first, which was completely understandable given the situation, but after getting to know him as a teen and then working with him as an adult, I found it laughable that I'd ever been afraid to be around him. He was an amazing man with a huge heart and a kind soul. He would give the shirt off his back to anyone in need, yet rarely shared any personal information about himself. I looked up at Matt as he looked out over the crowd with a small smile on his face and he smiled wider when he caught me looking at him.

"This is really something, isn't it?" I said.

"It sure is. It's still a bit mind-boggling that someone would take such an interest in my little center and want to help in such a big way. This new building will change everything," he replied.

"Well, they're a great group of people for sure, but I bet none of them would have fallen in love with the center if it wasn't for you and the work you're doing to improve the lives of those kids. You're the heart and soul of this organization," I told him, speaking passionately because it meant that much to me.

"I don't really do all that much. It's the kids who are the heart of the center," he replied modestly. I shook my head with a smile. That was typical Matt, always deflecting any attention given, away from himself.

I looked out over the room and smiled as I watched my friends. Giovanni and Caleb were kneeling on the floor talking animatedly to their daughter, Sarah, as if they were telling her a story. Carter had his hand in Ryan's back pocket as they talked to Lachlan and Rylie. Every so often, I'd see Ryan glance down at his husband, giving him a very heated look and I could only imagine what Carter was doing with that hand.

Landon and his husband, Micah, were talking with Landon's parents and I watched as Micah reached up and put his hand on the back of Landon's neck, letting him feel their connection. And then there was Morgan and Akio who were standing in a corner, talking quietly. Every once in a while, they'd glance down at the rings on their fingers and then give each other a look that was so intimate that I knew for them, they were the only two people in the room.

"I hope I find a love like that someday," I said wistfully, not referring to any one couple in particular. As far as I was concerned, they all had found the kind of love I'd like to have; the kind that lasts forever and defies all logic.

"I hope you do too," Matt murmured quietly and I thought I detected a hint of sadness in his voice. My heart squeezed at the thought of anything hurting Matt.

I glanced over at him and opened my mouth, but then shut it right away. I could tell that there was something in Matt's past that was haunting him and I wished that he would open up and let me in, but I knew, better than most, how painful it could be to revisit the past, so I let it go. I was still watching Matt when suddenly his back straightened and his eyes grew wide. He looked startled.

I turned my head to see what had caused his reaction and my heart skipped a beat when I saw the gorgeous man walking towards us. He was tall, even taller than Matt, with broad shoulders and biceps that would probably rip the sleeves of his shirt if he were to flex at all. He was wearing black dress pants, and a gray polo shirt, making him look both stylish and sophisticated.

He had beautiful ebony skin and full lips and his eyes were…his eyes were zeroed in on Matt and the look he was giving Matt could only be described as…hungry. I quickly looked at Matt and saw that his attention was still focused on the man. The look in Matt's eyes was a mixture of heat and confusion and something else that I wasn't quite sure of, but if I had to guess, I'd have to say…guilt?

My stomach knotted as I continued to watch the two men. There was an electric charge in the air that I'd felt on a few other occasions, but now it seemed stronger and I wasn't sure if it was coming from the two of them or if it was my own reaction.

Just as the stranger was about to reach us, he turned his eyes on me and those warm brown eyes widened just a fraction and then heated further. I could feel my body starting to respond to him, which surprised me because I had only ever reacted that way to one other man. His eyes bounced back and forth between Matt and me and he looked just as confused as I felt. When he was standing in front of us he spoke and his voice was rich and deep and it caused goose bumps to break out across my skin.

"Which one of you is Matt?" he asked.

"I am," Matt answered gruffly and then cleared his throat. He looked nervous and I could see sweat beading above Matt's brow. The stranger moved his head and my legs turned to jelly as I became the focus of his attention.

"Then you must be Isaac." He smiled, showing a row of perfectly straight teeth. It was a friendly smile, warm and inviting and my instincts kicked in, letting me know that he was safe.

"Yes," I said weakly. I tried to think of something else to add, but the synapses in my brain were too busy misfiring.

"It's nice to meet both of you," he said, sticking his hand out to shake first Matt's hand and then mine.

He stared at Matt as they shook hands, but Matt pulled away quickly, looking down at his hand as if he'd been shocked. He looked back up at the stranger in confusion. He shook mine next and I watched as his large hand engulfed my smaller one. It was warm and soft and I felt a current of electricity that traveled from my hand all the way up the back of my neck and out the top of my head. I looked at him in surprise and he was staring back at me, his head tilted to the side and I could see the questions behind those eyes. Unfortunately, I didn't have any answers as to what was going on.

I looked to Matt, because he'd always been the one I turned to, but his eyes were going back and forth between the stranger and myself. He paused on me and when he looked at me, it was as if he were seeing me for the first time. His tongue darted out to wet his lips and I felt a stirring in my groin. That wasn't anything new, but the way he was looking at me was. I felt off kilter and I wasn't sure what was going on with me or with Matt who had always been the strong and steady one of the two of us. Who was this man and what did he want?

"What's your name?" I asked. His brown eyes turned to me and my skin heated under his gaze.

"My name is Hudson."

The End

ACKNOWLEDGEMENTS

Thank you once again to my husband and my children. You three are my rock, my strength and my foundation upon which everything else is built. Everything I do is done with you three in mind and I hope I always make you proud.

To Deena, who has been there through all of the ups and downs, good days and bad and has remained steady and true through it all. I hope I am able to give you even half of the friendship that you've shown me.

To Kerry for always supporting me, encouraging me and being my biggest cheerleader throughout life. I am the luckiest girl in the world to have a sister like you.

To Aimee, for all of your enthusiasm, encouragement and putting up with my endless questions. I'm looking forward to working with you and seeing what crazy things we will come up with together.

To my amazing team: Pam Ebeler, thank you for your kindness, your expertise and your patience when dealing with my crazy. Thank you also for loving my guys almost as much as I do, sometimes to the point of late night, teary messages. LOL. I think you are remarkable and I'm very lucky to call you friend. Jay Aheer, thank you for your stunning creations. Time and time again, you take what I have only imagined in my mind and you bring it to life in the most beautiful ways. Thank you for your patience, your thoughtfulness and your friendship. Judy Zweifel, thank you for taking the time to make sure my books are the best they can be and for your patience and understanding. Stacey Blake, thank you for the time you spend adding in the extra touches that make my books so special. To my betas, Jodie Temple, Allison

Holzapfel, Lee Rey, Jenn Gibson, Melissa McIntyre, Nemerald, Lori Gries and Wendy Maples. Thank you for your willingness to read my story and for sharing such great feedback. Your encouragement, enthusiasm and friendship mean the world to me. You guys are all incredible and I couldn't do this job without each and every one of you.

ABOUT THE AUTHOR

I am married to my high school sweetheart who let's face it, is a saint for putting up with me all of these years. Together we have been blessed with the chance to raise two amazing human beings and so far we haven't screwed it up; I'll let you know for sure later. I am a business owner and spend more time laughing than actually working most days. I love watching movies, cooking, going to the beach and spending time with my family and best friends. I am an obsessive reader who is a complete sucker for a good love story, but loves to feel a broad range of emotions throughout a book. I think real life is hard enough and so my books offer twists and turns, but always with a happy ending.

I love to hear from my readers. You can reach me at:

Twitter
twitter.com/annabellamicha1

Facebook
www.facebook.com/profile.php?id=100011438515157

Annabella's Sexy Souls
www.facebook.com/groups/233274880449097

Blog
www.annabellamichaels.blogspot.com